$\mathcal{P}_{\text{raise for}}$

"I've never read her b—— —————— —— ———— — a half and my parents won't let me, but she seems like she would be a good writer."

—— —THE DAUGHTER OF TWO
CONSENTING ADULTS

"Darynda Jones is amazing! I've only read her most recent grocery list, but it was crazy! Strawberry AND chocolate cheesecakes? Bold choices!"

—— —CASHIER AT THE QUICKSTOP

"I do worry about her action-figure fetish. She seems so normal. I guess you never know."

—— —DARYNDA'S FIFTH GRADE TEACHER

Moonlight and Magic

BETWIXT AND BETWEEN BOOK 4

DARYNDA JONES

LIARS & THIEVES INK

MOONLIGHT AND MAGIC:

A PARANORMAL WOMEN'S FICTION NOVEL

(BETWIXT & BETWEEN BOOK 4)

©2022 by Darynda Jones

Cover design by Hang Le

EBook

ISBN 10: 1-954998-92-9

ISBN 13: 978-1-954998-92-6

Print

ISBN 10: 1-954998-99-6

ISBN 13: 978-1-954998-99-5

Sadly, all books have typos. Including this one. If you see any and would like to let us know, please email us at writerlyd-books@yahoo.com. THANKS SO MUCH!

www.DaryndaJones.com

Available in ebook, print, and audio editions

 Created with Vellum

You know who you are.
You know what you mean to me.
Thank you all for being in my orbit.

Introduction

Forty-something Annette Osmund always knew she was psychic. She's not, but that didn't stop her from giving those non-existent abilities her all. What she is, however, is a very powerful witch who has just inherited magics she never dreamed possible.

Starting over in a new town with her BFF has been an adventure. Her BFF's status as a powerful type of witch called a charmling has kept Annette busy. But while Defiance, a seeker, is still learning to use her magics, to control the power at her fingertips, Annette is overcome with powers of her own. Turns out, her being besties with Defiance was not an accident. They were drawn to each other even before their powers emerged, and Annette learns she is also a charmling, a healer and an alchemist. But how did this even happen?

Fortunately, there's one way to find out. She confronts her mother, because the only way she could be a charmling is to inherit the power, and her father, while a wonderful man, is hardly a magical being. But there is someone else who wants to know where she got her powers from as well: a delicious entity who's following her every move. She can either use her magics to try to shake him or learn to work with him, but working together could cost her the only thing she's kept safe for years: her heart.

Chapter One

I just asked myself if I'm crazy, and we said no.
—Meme

I stood on a deserted street and stared at my mother's front door as though I'd never seen it before. Mostly because I hadn't. She'd moved since I put Phoenix in my rearview almost seven months ago, and the red monstrosity that loomed like a giant mouth waiting to swallow me whole felt as foreign to me as pole-vaulting. Or shower sex. But it couldn't be helped. The conversation I needed to have with my mother could not be carried out over the phone.

I had questions.

Weighed down by luggage, a parka the size of Nebraska, and a Betsey Johnson handbag I bought with my last dime—because *Betsey Johnson*—I turned and watched as my Uber driver, my last hope of escape, faded into the distance. Metaphorically speaking. He actually made a left on Elm and

1

disappeared behind a mid-century duplex. Either way, if I'm being completely honest with myself, standing there watching my one and only contingency plan vanish was simply another form of procrastination. One of many I'd employed over the last couple of weeks. But I could no longer delay the inevitable. The time had come. No more dragging my feet. No more stalling. No more puttering or fiddling or—

"Essscuse me." A small voice emanating from somewhere on my right interrupted a very tenuous thought process. How many synonyms were there for procrastination?

I looked down at a kid on a trike, thankful for yet another reason to delay the inevitable discomfort hurtling toward me like a runaway train. The girl had glistening dark skin, two pigtails on the top of her head that stood up like antennae, and the most incredible set of eyes I'd ever seen. Rich amber irises framed in a centuries-old setting, full of curiosity and mischief and a hint of annoyance.

I was apparently blocking her path.

Wearing a rainbow tee, pink ruffled shorts, and sparkly cowgirl boots, she rocked her trike back and forth as though unable to sit still, even for a few seconds. Even now. Even with everything that had happened to her.

Being new to the whole seeing-dead-people thing, her presence startled me at first, especially when I noticed the skin scraped raw on one side of her face and down her left arm. While that gave me a good idea of how she died, a sadness settled in my chest with the knowledge. Aware we were still in the street, out in the open where anyone could see, I knelt down to her, ignored the creak in my knees, and offered her my very best smile. "What's your name?"

"Apple Ellen James the First, but Grandma Lou told me not to talk to strangers, so I can't tell you that."

I fought a grin. "The first, huh? That's quite an honor."

She lifted a slim shoulder. "Grandma Lou says I'm the first because I'm the only girl like me in our whole entire family."

I didn't doubt that for a minute. "I bet she thinks the world of you," I said, my heart melting.

"She lives in that house." She extended a tiny finger toward a similarly styled house next to my mom's. Red brick and multipaned windows, only her front door was a soft shade of sand. "And we used to live here," Apple added, swinging her arm to my mom's. "But we had to move, and now a crazy lady lives there with a man who smokes." She wrinkled her nose in disgust, and I tried not to laugh.

No wonder my mom could afford the place. She'd hooked up with someone new. Yet again. I could hardly blame the woman for trying to find her OTP, but she'd gone through five divorces in her six decades on Earth. There comes a time to accept defeat and become a cat lady. That was my plan, at least, especially since the man I was currently in love with died more than fifty years ago and was now haunting my BFF's house in Salem, Massachusetts. *C'est la vie.*

That being said, I did spot a hottie at the airport in Boston and then again on the flight over. Thick hair as dark as a starless night. What promised to be an exquisite jawline obscured by the upturned collar of a long black coat. The material, cut clean and clearly expensive, emphasized the massive expanse of his shoulders beautifully. But it was his eyes—a shimmering silvery blue—that made me forget how to breathe. At least during that brief glimpse I got before he disappeared around a corner at the airport or behind a passenger's seat on the plane. I looked for him almost desperately when we landed, my irises fairly begging for another peek, but with all the bustle of deboarding, I never saw him again. A pity because I couldn't help a niggling of familiarity in the back of my mind.

"I like your glasses," Apple said, pulling me out of my thoughts again, and I had to remember which pair I was wear-

3

ing. While almost always cat-eyed, my glasses tended to change colors with my mood. Today they were blue to help soothe the anxiety coursing through my veins.

"Thank you." Rising to my feet again, I hefted the parka and the Betsey Johnson onto a shoulder and took hold of my suitcase. Whoever invented wheels for these things deserved a Nobel Prize. Or a lifetime supply of frozen lasagna, because who doesn't love lasagna?

The minute I stepped out of her path, Apple rushed past me like she had someplace to be.

I called out to her. "Are you going to be around for a while?"

"Maybe," she said over her shoulder, pedaling to her grandmother's house with a fierce determination.

"Stay out of the street!" I yelled, though it was clearly too late for such warnings.

With a deep sigh, I turned back to my mother's front door and resigned myself to the inevitable. If the issue weren't so burning, if it weren't literally a matter of life and death, I wouldn't even bother. But this was no longer about me only. My BFF was a charmling, too, but at least her new title made sense. She'd been born into a family of witches.

I, on the other hand, had been born into a family similar in consistency and texture to the fruit in fruitcake. I'd never had a magical bone in my body, but suddenly I'm a charmling? Not just a witch, but a very powerful type of witch, one of only three in the world. And this was where it got sticky. This was why I needed my mother's help. A blood heir can only be born from a carrier of the magical gene. But the man I'd called *father* my entire life didn't have a magical bone in his body. Not that I knew of anyway. Depending on how this conversation went, he would be my next stop.

So many questions, so few steps to the front door. I listened to the rollers bounce in the grooves on the sidewalk as I made my way to Mom's new entrance. Only one car in the driveway, a brand-new Mercedes, so I hoped her new man wasn't home. But before I could knock, my phone rang.

I pulled it out of my bag and breathed another sigh of relief before answering my best friend's summons. Defiance was still in Salem, enjoying her new sweetheart and a new son she'd brought across from the other side, because apparently charmlings can do shit like that.

After tapping the green circle, I waited for her face to appear on my screen.

"Well?" she asked, her dark hair falling prettily around her face. She was sitting in the kitchen of her new, gorgeous mansion. A dilapidated Cape-Cod-esque manor named Percy any witch would be proud of.

"Well, what?"

"Did she tell you who knocked her up?"

I stuffed my coat through the telescopic handle on the suitcase. "I haven't seen her yet. I'm at her house now."

"Dude, you landed two hours ago."

"Have you already forgotten what traffic is like here?"

"Oh," she said, her tone deflating. "Sorry. Call me the minute you find out who your real dad is. Like that very second."

"You act like I'm on some grand adventure."

"You are! We talked about this. You'll always have your dad, and he'll always love you, but there is no way that man is a carrier of the charmling gene."

"I know, I know. I just don't think this conversation is going to be as easy as you're making it out to be."

"Annette Cheri Osmund. You've got this. Just pin those crazy curls to the top of your head and do what we talked about."

I took a deep breath and nodded. "Right. Lull her into an

innocuous conversation about the weather, then blindside her."

"Exactly. And don't give her a chance to retreat. You have a right to know who your real father is. And how the hell she hooked up with a witch. Or a warlock. Either way."

"True, but—" Before I could expound on the plethora of doubts running rampant through my brain, a tiny voice wafted into my ear, and my heart melted at the sweet sound.

"Hi, Aunt Netters!"

Defiance adjusted her phone to show the face of a blond-haired, blue-eyed Puritan wearing a Guns N' Roses T-shirt and a Stay Salty fisherman's hat. The little guy had officially been baptized in the modern era.

"Hi, Samuel," I said, cursing the pang of jealousy that spiked every time I saw the toddler. My best friend had rocketed from bankrupt divorcée to fiancée of the hottest journey-man-slash-werewolf I'd ever seen—not that I'd seen many—and mom seemingly overnight. And I was so happy for her, it hurt. Yet a tiny pang of envy pricked my heart, and I hated it. How could I be jealous of my best friend?

"Why you in that phone?" he asked, tapping the screen with his index. He may be wearing twenty-first-century garb, but he was still trying to figure out his new reality.

"I'm out of town," I said, laughing at the fact that he was essentially poking my face.

"Why you out of town?"

"That's a good question, but I'll be back—"

"Ink!" he cried before I could finish the sentiment, wiggling out of his mother's arms to chase a scruffy housecat named Ink. Poor creature. At least Samuel could no longer chase him through walls, so he did manage to eke out a few moments of peace in his otherwise frantic days.

"Oh, I saw a hottie in the airport," I said, changing the subject to something I knew Deph would love.

She turned the phone back to herself. "Yeah? Did you get his number?"

"Of course not. I couldn't just walk up to him and ask for his number."

"Why not? You used to do it all the time."

"Yes, as a joke. Also, I kept losing him."

"Darn."

"He looked strangely familiar, though. Like I've seen him recently, but I don't where from. Maybe—"

The door opened, and I stopped midsentence. Standing exactly half an inch shorter than me—we'd measured—my mother stood across the threshold, her short brown hair only slightly mussed, considering the hour. And she was still wearing a robe. A red one with candy canes on it. I decided not to ask.

"Annette?" she said, as though not sure it was me.

Had I changed that much? "Mom."

Her wary gaze slid past me, scanning the street for a car. Or my gang. "What are you doing here?"

I rolled my eyes. "I'm not here to rob you, Mom. Holy cow." I shoved past her to get out of the heat and came face-to-face with the daughter my mother never had, my cousin Krista.

Of course she would be here. Where else would she be?

"I'll call you back," I said into the phone.

"Wait!" Deph yelled as I hit the *end call* button. She had just enough time to stick out her tongue, and I almost laughed. Almost.

"What are you doing here?" Krista asked, as though worried she'd catch something.

My mom closed the door, and I looked between the two of them, suddenly at a loss for what to say. The last thing I wanted on this earth was for my cousin, the super popular one who used to squeeze toothpaste into

7

my hair as I slept, to find out I was questioning my ancestry.

And why the hell was she here? She and my mother used to do everything together. I thought their close relationship would ebb over the years, but it only seemed to grow stronger. The comparisons—or disappointments—grew stronger as well. Why couldn't I be more like Krista? Why couldn't I cheer like Krista? Why couldn't I paint like Krista? Why wasn't my hair soft and shiny and blonde like Krista's?

I was in my midforties, and that shit still stung like a tarantula wasp. I had to get over it already. Thank the goddesses for my bestie, Defiance. She'd kept me sane. Or at least she'd tried. The jury was still out.

"Oh," Krista said, eyeing the silver bracelets I'd woken up with that morning. Literally. I'd gone to bed with bare wrists and woken up with delicate silver vines around them. Not the oddest thing to happen to me in Defiance's new house, believe it or not. The fact that said bracelets had no clasps for me to take them off only added to their charm. Or creepiness. Either way.

"You should have called," my mother said, walking past me toward a kitchen that set off to the left.

I abandoned my suitcase in the foyer and followed. "I didn't realize I needed an appointment."

She turned to me in a huff. "That's not what I meant, Annie. I just moved into this house. I don't have a spare room ready."

"It's nice." I scanned the open area. White walls accented with soft woods. It was fancy. Especially for my mom.

"Thank you," she said, pouring a cup of coffee. "I can't wait for you to meet Brad."

"Pitt?" I asked hopefully.

Krista released a sound that was part laugh and part scoff. "Same old Annette."

"I've only been gone seven months, cuz. Did you expect me to change?"

"Not at all." She took a sip of her own coffee and headed toward the living room, saying over her shoulder, "But you can't have my room."

"Your room?" I asked, unable to hide my shock. "You live here?"

My mom handed me the cup. "She's just staying here while Daren is out of town."

I grinned at her. "Trouble in paradise already?" I asked, knowing the question would dig.

She whirled around. "At least I have a husband."

"Yes, you've had three," I reminded her, the words leaving my mouth before I had a chance to think it through.

A fury overtook my cousin, and I tried not to giggle at the fact that her lips took on a weird shape when she was mad, not unlike the Predator.

"Girls!" my mother scolded. Like always. She never curtailed Krista's digs, but the minute I got the upper hand, she'd put an end to our bickering with a single bark. It was simply the way of the world.

Our bickering really was childish, but my cousin brought out my inner fifth-grader like nobody's business. I was not afraid to pull hair.

"Sit down, Annie."

I sat on the closest thing I could find, a barstool covered in cow hide.

Mom and Krista sat beside each other on the sofa, then looked at me expectantly.

After taking a sip and examining my more immediate surroundings—my gaze pausing on a picture of my brother in a Little League uniform taken mere days before he disappeared —I said, "So, Mom, can we talk alone?"

"What did you do now?" she asked, the disappointment

on her face hitting that one nerve I'd reserved for special occasions. I suddenly no longer cared what my cousin thought. Of me or my mother.

"I didn't do anything. If it's not asking too much, however, I would love to know who my real father is."

Chapter Two

Hey, it's me, Pandora.
Welcome to my new unboxing video.
—Pandora's Point

(Please like and subscribe)

I'd never born witness to the whole pin-drop metaphor as much as I had in that moment. The room grew eerily silent as two of my most immediate relatives gaped at me, my cousin looking less *Predator* and more *Ghostface*.

"I beg your pardon," my mother said, coming to her senses first.

The cuz was still in shock.

Mom surged to her feet and glanced at her before her gaze bounced back to me.

I'd asked nicely. We didn't have to do this in front of Krista.

"What on earth are you talking about?" Mom asked.

I put my cup on the island behind me. "I know Dad is not

my biological father and, due to recent events, I really need to know who is. You understand," I added with a wink.

"Annette Cheri," she said through clenched teeth, her face turning an odd shade of purple. "Of course your father is your father. Why would you say such a thing?"

I started to argue, knowing full well that, as wonderful as my dad was, he did not contribute to my incubation in any way. It broke my heart, but if we were going to find out what was going on, why a charmling had been killed, reverting her powers back to a rightful heir—aka yours truly—we really needed to know whose sperm won the race that night.

"Mom," I said softly, knowing this was going to be hard for her. She'd always seemed so strong. So capable. Even when bouncing from man to man after my father divorced her—not long after my brother, Austin, disappeared—she never gave me a reason to question her strength. We always had food on the table and clothes on our backs. But seeing her now, the shock and raw emotion in her eyes... I was beginning to regret coming.

I almost said as much until a shadow drew my attention to the left corner of the living room. At first, I just blinked when I saw a man in a long black coat leaning against the wall, arms crossed over a wide chest like he hadn't a care in the world. Then I realized it was *the* man. The man from the airport. The man who'd been on the same flight from Boston, his hotness oozing into the room like molten lava as he watched me from beneath thick lashes, his expression partly guarded and partly amused.

I practically fell out of the chair, then looked between my mom, my cousin, and the man. My gaze rocketed back to my cousin. Had I ever met her latest husband? Was that him?

Both women turned to look at him, then back at me like I'd lost my mind.

No way was that her husband. No way was I this fucking

unlucky. But there was no denying it. My cousin was gorgeous. Always had been. Naturally she would attract a man who was just as gorgeous. No, even more so. As much as I hated myself for thinking this, he was a little out of her league.

When she looked at him again, then smiled back at me, she nodded and said, "Yep. Same old Annette."

I swallowed my disappointment, filled my lungs, and said, "I take it this is Daren?"

The name did not fit him. He looked about as much like a Daren as I—with my extra-curvy five-foot frame and brown labradoodle hair—looked like a Taylor Swift.

Mom and Krista once again looked at him then back at me. Then back at him. Then back at me. All in all, it was a weird exchange.

"I give up," Krista said, before picking up the remote. She turned the TV on and flipped to the local morning news as though ending the conversation, infuriating me even further.

I nodded a greeting to Daren, my heart aching with the knowledge that he was married to one of the most hateful people on earth yet dancing just a little knowing they were having problems. I was clearly going to hell, but her treatment of him could be a big clue as to why they were in a rough patch.

He nodded back, the same humorous grin lifting one corner of his mouth, the same wariness in his gaze as though he wasn't sure what to make of me. I could hardly blame him. I didn't know what to make of me either.

"So, Mom," I said, turning back to the woman who supposedly gave me life. I hated to do this in front of not one, but two other people, but there was no stopping now. "Any thoughts on who my father might be?"

Mom put her hands on her hips. A sure sign that she'd had just about enough of me, missy. "That is enough, Annette. This isn't funny anymore."

Was it funny before? I must've missed that part. "Mom, I'm not accusing you of anything. I just really, really, really need to know. Lives are at stake." And, as far as we knew, one was already gone. I walked over to an overstuffed chair that catty-cornered the sofa and sank into it, hoping Mom would follow.

She did. "What do you mean lives are at stake, Annette?"

I tried not to be swayed by the sharp tone in her voice. "Apparently, my biological father was... something else. Something... powerful. Are you afraid of him? Is that why you can't say?"

The more I spoke, the paler my mother grew. Even Krista noticed it. She took the remote to turn down the volume—her concern truly heartwarming—right as a story about a missing girl popped onto the screen.

"After an exhaustive search of the woods near the James' home, five-year-old Apple Ellen James is still missing, and her parents are asking anyone with information as to her whereabouts to call this number."

I lunged forward and wrenched the remote out of Krista's hands before she could lower the volume.

"Ouch," she said, pulling her hand back and cradling it, ever the drama queen. "Crazy much?"

"Do you know this little girl?" I asked Mom.

"No," she said, frowning at the screen. "Poor little thing. I heard she used to live in this house, but they moved a few miles away a couple of months ago. What are the odds of that?"

"I think her grandmother still lives next door," Krista said. Then she added caustically, "Why do you care?"

When I deadpanned her, she deadpanned me right back. That'd show me. But the ache in my heart for Apple's parents, for her Grandma Lou, knowing their hopes at finding their little girl alive were about to be destroyed, suddenly became overwhelming. I'd been there. I understood those emotions all too well, but I didn't know if it would be better for them to find her body now or to let them keep that hope alive for a little while longer. Which would hurt less?

I knew the answer, of course. They needed to know. They needed to find their daughter's body, and I knew the exact person who could help with that. "Excuse me," I said, rising to get my phone. "I need to make a call."

"Now?" Mom asked, confused.

"Sorry. I'll be right back." I turned to Daren and nodded again. "It was nice meeting you. Kind of. I guess." We didn't actually meet but...

Mom and Krista turned to him again, then looked at me for the third time like I'd lost my mind. I may be a little slow on the uptake, but all the clues were adding up. No one introduced us. Mom and Krista looked at the corner but quickly turned back without saying anything. He seemed to come out of nowhere.

Goose bumps erupted across my body, racing over my skin and up my spine as a wave of anxiety washed over me. He was something else. Was he a hunter? Or worse, a warlock? Had he put some kind of spell on them so they wouldn't acknowledge him?

I rose to my feet as nonchalantly as I could, walked to the kitchen, and grabbed the nearest knife I could get my hands on, which was a butter knife, so I ditched that one and hunted down a real knife, tearing through my mother's drawers. A steak knife would do. Or a butcher's knife. Or a machete.

Mom called out to me. "What are you looking for?"

I finally found the knife drawer and pulled out the biggest one I could find. Holding it out to him as I cornered the island, I asked, "Okay, mister man, what are you?"

He smirked at me. Smirked!

"Annette, what are you doing?" Mom asked, growing frustrated.

"I know how to use this," I warned him. "I went to chef's school."

"You took one cooking class," my cousin reminded me, "and you almost burned down your best friend's restaurant."

"But still," I said, easing closer, showing my most menacing side.

The man dropped his arms and put his hands in his pockets, so unimpressed it was insulting.

"Annette Cheri, are you on new medication?"

"Who is he, Mom?"

"Who is who? There is no one there." She showed me her palms and stepped forward slowly as though approaching a wounded animal.

I gaped at him. "You made them unable to see you? Is that how you got in here with no one noticing?"

He only tilted his head and studied me, his shimmering gaze more menacing than I was comfortable with.

After reasserting my power over him by waving the knife, he obliged by raising a single brow. I scoffed. "And here I thought you were handsome. You're a warlock, aren't you?"

He tipped an invisible hat, and my body went cold. He really was a warlock? I didn't know much about warlocks, but I knew they were powerful. And although I was a charmling, warlocks were infamous for enslaving my kind.

Then again, they were not blood heirs like Defiance and me. Surely he couldn't do something like that to us, but why else would he be here? We'd already stopped one hunter—a warlock's servant—from claiming me for his boss. Had said boss come for me himself?

The sound of laughter wrenched my attention toward my cousin, and I remembered they couldn't see him. I must've looked crazy. Well, I always looked crazy, but I must've looked crazier than usual.

"Excuse me," she said, picking up her phone. "I have to tell every person I've ever met what is happening. Freak."

"Krista, stop it," my mother hissed at her, and it caught us both by surprise. Mom never chastised the *chosen one*.

Krista turned a pretty pout on her.

"Annie," Mom said, again as though talking to a wounded animal, trying to convince it she'd come in peace. She turned back to the corner, then slowly put some distance between the warlock and herself.

"Can you see him?" I asked her.

"No, honey, I can't, but I know how tricky they are."

The warlock turned his gaze on my mom, pressing a hand over his heart and feigning a hurt expression.

I knew the knife would do no good whatsoever, but I felt better having it. I waved it at him again, luring his gaze back to me.

"Aunt Dolores, are you seriously entertaining her delusions?"

I pulled Mom until she was behind me and then started backing toward the door. I was absolutely helpless against a warlock. I knew little to no spells, despite studying day and night for two weeks, the length of time since I'd inherited my charmling powers.

Then I remembered: I could shapeshift. Thanks to my bestie turning me into a danged bird—a crow to be exact—I could fly away once I got outside. Surely he couldn't follow me. Even if he could shapeshift, what were the odds his alternate form could fly?

But I couldn't leave him alone with my mom. Krista could fend for herself. My mom, not so much. Then again, what would he want with her? Would he leave her alone if I escaped?

We'd made it to the foyer. The warlock hadn't moved a muscle, his gaze unwavering, and I started to breathe a hairs-breadth easier when my mother's words sank in. "Wait, what?" I asked her, turning toward her.

"What what?" she asked, her gaze darting about madly as though trying to see into the beyond. "Why are you whating me? Keep that knife on him."

"Is this a joke?" Krista asked as she lifted her phone to film us.

"You said warlocks were tricky. How would you know that?"

She stopped and gave me her full attention. "Can we discuss this outside?"

"How do you know that, Mom?"

"This is so going viral," Krista said right as her phone started to smoke. She yelped and dropped it on the coffee table, shattering the screen. "What the hell?"

Mom went still beside me. "Did the warlock do that?"

I turned wide-eyed to the man. He gave his right shoulder the barest hint of a shrug, as though he'd been helpless against the urge to fry my cousin's phone.

I liked him. Not a lot, but he was growing on me. "I think he did."

Krista waved smoke away from her face as her phone continued to smoke. "This is a brand-new phone and I didn't get insurance."

"That's so sad," I said before turning back to my mom and asking her point-blank, "How do you know warlocks are tricky?"

"We can discuss this later."

"Mom, how do you know?" I pressed, keeping the knife trained on the intruder.

She let out a helpless sigh and closed her eyes. "Because I think your father may have been one."

"What?" Krista and I said at the same time.

"My biological father was a warlock and you never told me?"

She clutched at my arm, practically begging me to pay attention to the elephant in the room instead of her. "I'm not saying he was for sure, but... I saw things, Annie. Things I can't explain. That being said, can we get back to the warlock in my house?" Her fearful expression returned as she scanned the room. "Is he still here?"

"Yes," I said toward the warlock, as though accusing him of wrongdoing. He was a warlock, after all. He'd probably done lots of things wrong in his life, so my animosity was warranted. He was so young, though. He couldn't have been more than thirty. Maybe thirty-five, but that was pushing it.

"The man who came to me was terribly handsome."

"Like, dark-hair handsome with shoulders that went on for miles and piercing blue eyes?"

The warlock ducked his head to hide a grin, and the dimples that appeared on either side of his mouth did not cause my stomach to somersault. It was the situation. I was nauseous from the adrenaline coursing through my veins.

"Yes," Mom said, then amended her statement. "Wait, no. My warlock was blond with brown eyes. It's not the same one." She relaxed her grip on my arm, though just barely.

Krista went into the kitchen and came back with an oven mitt. "I have to get to the wireless store before work." She picked up her phone with the mitted hand, grabbed her bag off a side table with the other, and strode past us. "After that, I'm calling the people in white to come get the both of you." She slammed the door behind her, and I watched the warlock.

He couldn't have cared less that she left.

"Mom, I need you to get your keys and go."

"What? No, honey. I can't leave you."

"Mom, please."

19

"And I haven't put my makeup on."

"Mother," I said in warning.

"Okay." Without another thought, Mom ran to her room as I kept the knife trained on my target. For, like, a really long time.

He watched me, and I watched him, and I swore I heard elevator music playing in my head as we waited. And waited. And waited. No matter. It gave me a chance to study him even further. I wanted to memorize that face. That chiseled mouth and jaw. The straight nose and razor-sharp eyes spilling over with a shimmering blue. The thick hair as dark as a starless night. Those wide shoulders and long arms. I concentrated on memorizing every part of him should I need to describe his features to a sketch artist. That was absolutely the only reason I would ever do such a thing.

When Mom finally hurried out of her room wearing a sundress and flip-flops, I looked at the clock. She'd only been in there for about three minutes, but it seemed so much longer. "Is he still there?" she asked.

"He is. Just get in your car and go."

"It's in the garage."

"Okay," I said, wondering what that had to do with anything. "Is that a problem?" I asked over my shoulder.

"It's just that the door you're looking at is the door to the garage."

I realized there was indeed a door right beside the warlock. Crap on a cracker. "Can't you go outside and open the door from there?"

She cowered against my backside, gazed over my shoulder, and whispered, "I could if I knew the code."

I dropped the hand holding the knife and gaped at her, whispering back, "You don't know the code?"

"We just moved in last week. I have an opener. I haven't learned it yet."

The long, drawn-out sigh I released sounded very much like a dying cow, but I didn't care. I formed a plan and retrained the knife on the intruder. "Okay, you," I said, jabbing the knife toward the other side of the room. "Go over there so my mom can get out."

He pointed to himself and raised his brows.

"Yes, you. Who else would I be talking to? And don't try anything funny. I know spells. I can"—I had to think fast, not my strong suit—"I can send you to an oblivion so... oblivious you'll never be able to find your way out."

He raised his brows again, this time pretending to be impressed.

I was so bad at acting. I pointed with the knife to my right. "Whatever, just go that way."

He pointed to the other side of the room with a long, almost elegant finger. Damn it. He even had great hands.

"Yes, yes," I said, waving the knife like a maniac. "That way. Walk over there."

At last, he raised his hands in surrender and strolled to the other side of the room, taking up his new post in front of a sliding glass door. That wasn't the odd part. The odd part was the fact that I could see daylight streaming through him. How? Was he not really there? Was he astral projecting or something? Could warlocks do that? If so, I doubted I could outrun him even as a bird.

"Go, Mom," I said, pushing her away from me.

"What are you going to do?" she asked.

"I have a few tricks up my sleeve," I lied.

"Tricks? What kind of tricks?"

"Mom, I'm the daughter of a warlock. I can handle this."

"Is this what you and Defiance have been doing in Salem? Learning the black arts?"

"Really, Mom?" I asked, appalled. "I just wrangled you a

get-out-of-jail-free card. Go already." I shooed her with my knife hand.

"All right, but we are going to talk about this later, young lady."

"Hell yes, we are." Why was she mad when I was the one who'd been lied to my entire life? "And a lot of other things, too."

Mom hurried through the door after taking one last glance at me as though it would be her last. Did she know something I didn't? Besides who my real dad was?

Alone at last with Mr. Tall, Dark, and Deadly, I waited until I heard the garage door closing before turning my attention to him. I swallowed hard and asked, "Why are you here?"

He spread his hands in a shrug. Why wasn't he talking? "Why aren't you talking?" Maybe warlocks couldn't talk when they astral-projected. "Can you not talk because you've astral-projected?" I glanced at the ceiling in thought. "Projected astrally?"

He tilted his head to the side as though fascinated by something. Probably my grasp of the English language.

Before I could think of another question to ask, aka, waste time while I figured out if I could shift into a bird or not, a car horn sounded out front. I looked through one of the glass panels beside the door and saw my mom sitting on the street in front of the house, honking for me. Goddess bless that woman.

The question remained: Should I try to shift to get away from him? I'd only done it two times, once when Deph changed me and once when I was practicing, but it took me three hundred tries to accomplish it. While I did manage it, I was scared I'd get stuck, so I didn't practice any more.

Even if I could shift, I wouldn't be able to get out the front door without opposable thumbs. Thus, I started backing toward the door, keeping the knife at the ready while watching him like a hawk. When I felt the doorknob at my back, I straightened my knife arm to prove to him I wasn't afraid to use it, then reached around with my free hand and opened the door.

He simply stood there staring at me, a roguish kind of humor playing about his mouth. Goddess, he had a nice mouth.

Once the door opened behind me, I bolted. I sprinted down the walkway and practically dove into her dark blue crossover. The one with tan seats. The tan seats that I slashed with the knife while jumping in. I gasped, but Mom didn't seem to care. Thankful I didn't stab her, I slammed my door shut and shouted, "Floor it, Mom!"

Chapter Three

The great thing about my soul is that
black goes with everything.
—Meme

Mom broke the sound barrier heading out of the quaint cul-de-sac and didn't stop until we had to. A warlock. An actual practitioner of the black arts. And he'd somehow found his way to my doorstep. Or, well, one I'd recently been on.

"Seatbelt," Mom said as she panted, waiting for the light to turn green.

I dropped the knife and my purse onto the floorboard and struggled to fasten my seatbelt. Once I managed it, I leaned back into the seat and focused on not hyperventilating. Coming here alone was a bad idea, but how did a warlock find me so fast? No, how did a warlock find me at all? Defiance had done a spell to cloak me. No one in the world of magics should've been able to feel my powers. Powers that I wasn't even close to being able to control.

According to legend, I was an alchemist. *Of tawdry and taint*, one book said. A mortiferata who could kill with a kiss. Cool? Yes. Scary as all get out? Even more so. And yet, if I had to, I could kiss the warlock. Surely that would get him out of my life. Or I could have if he were corporeal. Maybe that's why he wasn't. Maybe he was scared of my deadly kiss.

Probably not, though. I didn't strike fear in the hearts of many.

The light changed, and Mom went through the intersection only to turn into a grocery store parking lot. She put the car in park, turned it off, and turned to glare at me. "Why is a warlock following you around, Annette?"

Back to being angry, I pinned her with my best glower. "Because, Mother," I said as caustically as I could, "I'm apparently the daughter of one, and now I've come into my powers and I just want to live my life without poisoning my friends or blowing anyone up, but because I had no idea I even had powers, I have no way of controlling them, thank you very much, and who is my biological father?"

She sat blinking at me for a solid minute, getting us nowhere fast.

"Mom," I said, my tone softer because her gray eyes were clouding over with something I couldn't identify, "just tell me. Who'd you hook up with?"

She diverted her gaze by looking out the window. "I don't know. I don't... remember. I was at a bar with some friends and..."

After a long moment, I prodded with a soft, "And?"

It took her a few minutes to find her voice again. When she did, it trembled with emotion. "I was dating your dad at the time. I mean, Joe."

Joseph Osmund. The man I'd always believed to be my real father.

"But the girls had gone to the bathroom, and this man

came up to me. He was so..." A delicate hand covered her mouth as she thought back. "He was so startlingly beautiful. He didn't even have to say anything. I wanted him more than I wanted air. He took my hand, kissed the back of it, and that was the last thing I remembered."

"Wait, he didn't talk to you?" Was that just a warlock thing? I'd never met one until very recently.

"Not that I remember."

A cold sense of dread crept over me. "Are you absolutely certain he wasn't tall and gorgeous with inky black hair and shimmering blue eyes?"

She shook her head. "Not at all. He was blond. And I remember thinking his eyes were brown, they were so dark. In the low lights of the pub, they actually looked black."

I breathed a sigh of relief. Surely the warlock I'd seen could not have been my father. Not that it mattered, I supposed. He was still a warlock. "What do you mean, that's all you remember?"

"I woke up in my bed the next morning. I didn't remember leaving the pub. A few weeks later, I found out I was pregnant."

"Mom," I said on a soft gasp as her meaning sank in. I turned to look out my window, the disgust billowing inside me overwhelming. "So, my biological father is a rapist. Great."

"I don't know, Annie. I just don't remember."

"I promise you, he did that on purpose." I curled my hands into fists and dug my fingernails into my palms to relieve some of the anger surging inside me. "From what little I know about them, it's what they do. They're unscrupulous."

"Oh," she said in a small voice.

Then another thought hit me. "Wait, does Dad know? That I'm not his biological daughter?"

"Goodness, no." She turned the car back on to run the AC, and I noticed the wetness on her pale cheeks. I'd never seen her fragile. Fragile was not her style. It shook me more than I'd expected. "I never told him about that night. I never told anyone. Not even my girlfriends who wondered where I'd gone."

I could only imagine why. It must've been awful to find out she was pregnant after she'd technically been roofied, albeit most likely with a spell of some kind. How horrible. And yet... "You kept me," I said, surprised.

"Of course I did, Annette. Your dad—Joe—"

"Dad," I corrected, suddenly feeling rather asslike.

"Your dad took responsibility immediately, even though we'd only fooled around once. He insisted we get married, and it was good at first. Really good. Then your brother came along, and I just felt so whole. So fulfilled. Like I never had in my life." Her gray eyes shimmered with unspent tears. "And then..."

I put a hand on her shoulder. I would never forget the day Austin went missing. The police cars. The news vans. The lights shining in our house at all hours. And my parents crying nonstop. For days and days and days.

My chest tightened painfully around my heart. "I'm so sorry, Mom. I don't know if I've ever told you that, but I am. I was not a very good daughter then."

Mom's gaze darted toward me, and she stared at me a solid minute before she spoke. "Annette Cheri, you were a kid. You were hurting, too. We never blamed you."

I winced at the lie that came so easily to her. "He went missing on my watch. I understand your animosity now. I understood it then, too, even though I couldn't admit it at the time."

She turned in her seat to face me, reached over the console, and took my hand into hers. It was unexpected and almost unwelcome. I didn't deserve kindness from her. Animosity felt better. Normal. Like it was our schtick and I didn't know how to act otherwise. "Annette," she said, her tone softening, "I never felt animosity toward you. Nor did your father."

"It's okay, Mom."

"No, it's not. We were not the best parents, I'll give you that, but we never blamed you, honey. I guess..." She sniffed and drew in a deep breath. "I guess we should have told you that a long time ago."

It wouldn't have made a difference if they had. I was not a fool. They did blame me. At least my mother did, even if only just a little. I'd left Austin in front of the TV one Saturday morning to take a shower, and when I came out, he was gone.

It was all so blurry now. The frantic search. The phone call to the store where my mom clerked. To the garage where my dad worked. I'd never forget them running through the front door. Scouring the area. Calling out to him. Mom shaking me in front of our neighbors, screaming in my face. This was back when it was normal to leave nine-year-olds home alone to watch their younger siblings. No one blinked an eye.

That was when I first started believing in the crazy notion that I was psychic. I kept telling everyone Austin was alive. I could feel it. I knew it in my bones. But after weeks of searches and flyers and news appearances begging for information with nothing to show for it, even I was beginning to doubt my connection to him.

And then it all stopped. Almost as quickly as it began, it all stopped. The searches. The news vans. The two detectives who practically lived at our house. It all stopped and, after a few shaky starts, life began anew. We were just expected to go on living like we hadn't been through the worst thing that could ever happen to a family.

But nothing was ever the same. My parents got a divorce a year later. Mom and I moved to a new school district. Then, a few years after that, it was gone. My connection to Austin, the one I believed in with all my heart, was gone. I'd truly lost him.

I shook out of my thoughts and remembered something else she'd mentioned. "You said warlocks are tricky. That you'd seen things, but you don't remember that night?"

She bowed her head in thought, and I could tell she didn't want to talk about it, but we'd made so much progress. I didn't want to stop now.

"I don't remember that night, but afterward, I began having flashes. Visions. I can't explain it exactly. I just knew it was him, and I knew, somehow I knew he was a warlock." She refocused on me, her expression haunted. "Like he got off on taunting me. On scaring me." She shivered at the thought.

Heat rose inside my chest, and I had to fight to keep from grinding my teeth to dust. "If I ever find him, Mom, he will pay."

"No." She clutched my hand tighter. "No, honey. Please don't look for him. He's not normal."

I put my free hand over hers. "I'm not normal either, Mom. Neither is Defiance. You should see her." My BFF was something else. I suddenly couldn't wait for my mom to see her now. To see what she was capable of. What I could be capable of if I could stop trying to poison the people around me and/or blowing things up. I had to get a handle on my powers, and fast, thus my search for my biological father.

That search, however, just came to a screeching halt now that I was one hundred percent certain he was most definitely a warlock. I'd figured he could just be a regular guy who carried the charmling gene, completely unaware of the powerful line he'd descended from. No way was I hunting down an actual warlock on my own. Eff that. I needed some help, and I knew an entire coven I could recruit to my cause.

Before Mom could reply, the volume on the radio shot up to deafening levels. We covered our ears and turned to it in surprise. It was a news segment about Apple.

"The search continues for the missing five-year-old after

searches failed to find any clues as to her whereabouts. The family is offering…"

The words faded away as I caught a darkness in my periphery. I realized why my mom's crossover had turned into Christine. The radio was being controlled by a handsome warlock who was currently sitting behind my mother in the back seat.

I stilled when our eyes met, not sure what to do. Our gazes stayed locked for a few frozen seconds before my fight-or-flight kicked in. And for some inane reason, it chose fight. What the hell? I'd only been in one fight in my life, and I got my ass kicked. In my defense, I was seven and my opponent was twelve. And male. But he'd been picking on my little brother.

I lunged for the knife on the floorboard, straightened with enough dramatic flair to light up Las Vegas, and held it out to him while scooting as far into the dashboard as I could manage. "Mom, get out of the car!" I yelled over the sound.

She didn't hesitate. She opened her door and practically fell out while I fumbled blindly for my door handle.

The intruder showed his palms and pointed to the radio with his chin.

The sound lowered to a manageable volume as he watched me.

"If you have any information, please call the one eight hundred—"

"Annie!" my mom called. "Get out of the car!"

I spared her a quick glance, her expression filled with terror, and I swore right then and there I would hunt down my biological father after all, for doing that to her. For putting that kind of fear into her. But first, I needed to deal with the entity in the back seat. "Why are you here?"

We were beginning to get onlookers. A couple of people slowed their carts to check out the commotion like rubbernecking shoppers.

My fingers wrapped around the door handle, and I

debated the whole fight-or-flight thing again. The warlock lowered his hands and watched me.

"Why are you here?"

He pursed his lips as though disappointed in me right before the radio went staticky. It scrolled through station after station and stopped on another news story about Apple James.

I frowned at him. "Apple? You're here for Apple?" My blood ran cold when I put two and two together. To come up with forty-seven, apparently. "Did you take her?"

The indignant glare he shot me would suggest he did not.

"Then what?" I listened to the story, which said the exact same thing as the previous one, my fingers aching to pull the door handle. To run for my life, but the man could clearly show up wherever he wanted whenever he wanted. Would running do any good? Then realization dawned, hitting me like a lightning strike. "You want me to help her family?"

When he gave me a single determined nod, I gaped at him, appalled.

"I can't help them. How could I possibly help them? Unless you want me to put them out of their misery because I have a habit of turning edible items into poisonous ones. I'm fairly good at that."

He tilted his head as though waiting patiently for me to catch up.

"Wait. Defiance. She's the finder of lost things. Is that what you mean? You want me to ask Defiance to find Apple's body?"

He lifted a shoulder as though saying, *Whatever works.*

I shook my head, utterly confused. "Why? I mean, you're a warlock, right? Are you needing a body for a ceremony of some kind, because ew."

His mouth slid to one side of his face, clearly annoyed, though the act did nothing to detract from his insanely good

31

looks. It merely deepened one dimple, and I clenched my teeth in annoyance right back at him. Seriously, the guy had won the genetics lottery. It was not fair. He was a bad guy. All warlocks were. At least, that was my understanding. Why did he get to be so good-looking? And what else could a warlock want with the body of a poor little girl who just wanted to visit her grandmother?

"Then what?" I asked as my phone rang.

I didn't spare a glance for my purse on the floorboard, deciding my life was worth ignoring a call or two. When the ringtone only got louder and louder—louder than a phone had a right to be—the warlock lifted a brow as though waiting for me to pick up.

"Is that you?" I asked, still too scared to take my eyes off him.

"Annette!"

I nodded toward my poor mom, letting her know I was okay. For the time being.

He didn't answer, of course, so I shifted the knife into my left hand, which was actually my more dominant. His life was now in even more danger and he had no clue what awaited him should he make a move for me. Probably a whole lot of screaming on my part since he was basically air, but I felt better with the knowledge.

I reached into the area at my feet. My fingers slid over my purse strap, and I pulled it onto my lap. The ringtone was louder than the phone was even capable of. I pulled it out of a side pocket just as the ringing stopped. But the screen wasn't lit up. I didn't get a call.

When I looked back at him, confused, he offered me the barest hint of a smile.

My phone dinged, this time with a text. But the text wasn't attached to a number. Instead, three skulls with crossbones emojis popped up as the sender. I tapped the screen. It simply read, *Find her.*

A bright red pickup screeched to a stop beside the crossover, and a scraggly man with skinny bowed legs jumped out. He first looked through the windshield as though searching for someone then scanned the area. When his gaze landed on my mother, he rushed over to her.

"Brad!" she cried and practically fell into his arms.

Oh. So that was my new dad. At least this week. The unkempt guy looked like he'd ridden one too many bulls. Moved like it too, the stiffness in his limbs obvious.

My phone rang, and I turned back to the warlock only to find an empty back seat. I turned back to my phone and breathed a sigh of relief. "Defiance, you will not believe—"

"I've been trying to call you for an hour!

"What? My phone hasn't rung."

"What's wrong? I can feel something is wrong."

"You can feel it? Is that new?"

"Not really. Kind of. Ever since you came into your powers, I think I've been getting your emotions mixed up with my own."

It made sense. I'd been doing something similar. "So that's where the insatiable happiness I've been feeling has been coming from. You."

"Really? You can feel my happiness?"

"'Parently," I said, trying not to be disappointed. I thought I was happy despite my inability to control my powers. Turns out I was siphoning happiness off my bestie like a leech. I fought a traitorous smile. It wasn't like I could really be disappointed. My best friend was happy after years of misery. How could I be disappointed?

"Wait, can you feel... other things?" The minute she dropped her voice, I knew what she meant.

"Every single time." When the phone went completely silent, I giggled. "Not really. Thank the goddess."

Deph released a long breath of air she'd been holding in. "Thank the goddess, indeed. Do you know how awkward that would be?"

"Yes, I do." Dodged a bullet there.

"Wait, why are you upset? Is your mother being mean? Do I need to come down there?"

I laughed. "Actually, my mother and I had the first real heart-to-heart we've ever had."

"Oh, Nette, that's awesome. And?"

"Turns out my father is not only a warlock, but a sexual predator. He assaulted my mother. After he magically roofied her."

"No," she said softly. "I am so sorry, hon."

"Thank you. Though she doesn't remember much, it really affected her." I shook my head. "But I can't get into that right now."

"Of course. Is she close by?"

I looked over. Her new beau had sat her on a curb underneath a tree. "Close-ish, but someone followed me here."

"Someone followed you?" She gasped aloud. "The hunter?"

There'd been a hunter—basically a warlock's bitch—looking for me in Salem before I left, but we'd come to an understanding. He doesn't try to recruit me for his asshat of a warlock—who'd already enslaved the last of the three charmlings—and we don't fry him up and serve him to Defiance's familiar, Olly.

"Not a hunter," I said, knowing what I was about to say would send her into a tailspin. "Someone much more powerful, but you can't freak out."

"If you say a warlock, I am most definitely freaking out."

"No! Not a warlock. Not a warlock at all. Not a warlock in

any way, shape, or form, except that, yes, a warlock, only not like you think. He doesn't seem evil."

"Annette! How else can someone be a warlock? I mean, you're either a warlock or you're not. You're either evil or you're not. There's no middle ground here."

"Not true. Remember, Gigi said some can be benevolent. And he seems kind of nice."

"Oh my God." I could just see her pinching the bridge of her nose. "Is he hot?"

"What does that have to do with anything?"

"Nette, if he's a warlock, he's evil. I've been studying. There've only been three warlocks known for their benevolence in all of our history. In hundreds and hundreds of years. You've got to put your hormones aside for five minutes."

"Excuse me, Ms. I Think I'll Just Bang the Hot, Kilt-Clad Shapeshifter on the Kitchen Counter, but I think you are getting us confused."

"How did you—? Look, that doesn't matter. My hot, kilt-clad shapeshifter isn't a warlock." She paused for dramatic effect, then added, "A warlock, Annette! A bona fide master of the black arts. The same black arts that, if I may remind you, can enslave you for all eternity."

I rolled my eyes so far back into my head I felt a little seasick. Or maybe that was just the events of the day. "You're being melodramatic. I won't live for all eternity. And I already thought of the whole enslavement thing, but for some reason he only wants me to find a missing girl's body."

That perked her up. "A missing girl's body? What missing girl's body? And why would a warlock want you to find a missing girl's body? Though that does sound rather warlocky. There are necromancers out there."

"Yeah, I read that, too. I'm not sure why he wants me to find her body, but there are a few things about him I don't understand."

"Just a few?"

"He's not corporeal." When Deph didn't answer for a few seconds, I explained, "That means he's incorporeal."

"I know what it means."

"Just making sure. Can warlocks, like, astral project or something?"

An older voice, feminine and sweet, answered from what seemed like a few feet away from Deph. "Only the most powerful ones," her grandmother said.

"Hey, Gigi."

"Oh, I had you on speaker," Deph said.

"Yeah, I got that," I said, almost giggling. "He doesn't seem to be able to talk, but he must be really powerful. He can appear out of nowhere and control electronics. Maybe when they are incorporeal, they can't talk?"

"I don't know, Sarru," Gigi said, using the title the coven gave Deph and me. "What does he look like?"

"That's just it. He looks strangely familiar. Pitch black hair. Blue eyes as blue as, well, Defiance's. And, yes, he is very, very good-looking, but that has nothing to do with my assessment. He's just really intent on me finding Apple's body. Do you know why, Gigi?"

Gigi didn't answer for a very long time. I even checked my phone to make sure we were still connected. I heard muffled voices in the background, and then Gigi came on at last.

"Annette," she said, her voice soothing like elevator music, or morphine, "you need to come home as soon as possible."

"Oh, okay. Should I be worried?"

"Not at all, hon, but a warlock sniffing around, corporeal or not, is nothing to sneeze at."

"No sneezing. Got it. In the meantime, Deph, can you find the girl's body? I met her, and I'd really like to help her family find closure."

"Of course. I'm looking now. Apple James?"

"That's her."

"Oh, Nette, she's beautiful. You met her?"

"Yes, outside my mother's new house. Mom shacked up with someone new, by the way, but at least they have a really nice crib." Either the doctor she was working for was paying my mother very well or, despite the looks of him, Brad had a really good job.

"Please don't say crib again unless you're having a baby."

"Sorry. Do you think you can find her body?"

"I can try. I'll need all the information you have and, not to sound morbid, but do you know how she died?"

"I can't be certain, but I think it was a hit-and-run. She has road rash something terrible."

"Poor baby. This is breaking my heart. Okay, I'll do my best."

"Thanks, Deph."

"Annette, where is the warlock now?" Gigi asked in her super-soothing voice again. Something was definitely up.

"He's gone. He just appears and disappears, but he definitely followed me from Salem. I saw him at the airport and then again on the plane."

"He was on the plane?" Deph asked, surprised.

"Yes, but he disappeared around a corner and I never saw him deboard. Do you think he somehow materialized on the plane?"

"Maybe, but why do that?"

"That's the one-hundred-thousand-dollar question." I glanced over at my mom. Her new beau was helping her back to the car. "Gotta go. Let me know if you find her."

"Of course. Text me every half hour or I'm flying out there. I mean it, Nette."

"I will. Promise." I ended the call and took one last glance into the back seat before getting out of the car to help with Mom.

Her beau looked like he'd been a cowboy in his younger days. He wore a denim shirt and threadbare jeans. His appearance surprised me. He didn't match the house they'd gotten together. Maybe that was more my mom's decision than his. And while I was normally a big fan of scruffy, there was something off about the guy. He gave me a very bad vibe the minute I saw him, and I was suddenly worried about my mom. Where did she find these guys?

He helped my mom with a hand on her arm and one on her back.

"Brad, this is Annie," Mom said, as though proud to introduce me. Another novel experience. This day just kept getting weirder and weirder.

Brad gave me a dismissive nod, then looked down at her. "Your daughter can drive your car home. I'll take you with me."

"Do you mind?" Mom asked.

"Of course not. The keys in the car?"

"Yes. Is it... clear?"

After a furtive glance at Brad, not sure what all she told him, I said, "It is."

She nodded and leaned inside to grab her bag. Handing me the keys, she added, "She's kind of temperamental in this heat, but it should be okay. You have the address, right?"

"She has the address," Brad said, his impatience, and unmistakable dislike, shining through in the tone of his voice.

That was okay. He wasn't making a great first impression on me either.

He pointed to his truck that was still running, the big motor rumbling around us. The lift kit would make it hard for my mother to get in. The side steps would help, but that thing was, like, five feet off the ground.

Mom walked around to the other side. After she disappeared around the massive truck, Brad turned back to me. He gave me a good once-over, making me crave a long, hot shower. Then he closed the distance between us, wrapped his fingers around my upper arm, and jerked me toward him.

In a few minutes, I would begin rehearsing this situation in my head over and over, and would probably continue to do so for years to come. But at that moment, I was so stunned I just stood there gaping at him.

When he spoke, he was so close I could see the flakes of dry skin across his cheeks and the yellow stains on his teeth. I could also smell the cigarettes on his Bob Seger T-shirt and breath. How could someone so vile wear such a cool T-shirt? I figured he looked older than he actually was. He'd lived hard and it showed. "Look, I get it," he said, his voice low yet razor sharp. "It's fun. You've hated your mom for years so you decide to mosey back into town to scare the shit out of her."

Even though he had a viselike hold on my arm, I wrenched it out of his grasp, immediately regretting it when pain shot down my arm. "Yes," I said, refusing to rub it or take a step back. "That is exactly why I flew all the way from New England to the Southwest. To scare my mom. Because I'm a child."

"How about you call a cab when we get back to the house? Your mother has been through enough without you filling her head with ridiculous thoughts of witches and warlocks."

She'd told him a lot in those few minutes.

He spun on a heel to leave but turned back for one final disapproving glare. "And maybe you should join the twenty-first century. I'd hate to see you burned at the stake."

Did he just threaten me? Holy shit. Toxic much? And his warning made no sense. If I were in danger of being burned at the stake, I would be in another century altogether.

All in all, our little interaction had me wondering three things. Why was he with my mother when they were polar opposites? Why was he chomping at the bit to get rid of me?

And how much insurance had he taken out on her life? Three things I planned to find out very soon.

I watched him walk away, his stick-thin frame sturdy despite the bony edges and too-sharp angles of his body. He climbed into that massive truck like a pro, then roared out of the parking lot.

My phone dinged with a text from the warlock. After a quick scan of the area, I opened it, read it, then swirled around looking for him harder, even bending to look in the car. When I didn't see him, I reread the text. It said simply, *Dead man walking.*

Chapter Four

*My personality is that one drawer in the kitchen
that's just full of random stuff.*
—Fact

After making a pit stop for some convenience store coffee, I
made my way back to my mom's house. Before I got out, I
decided to take my relationship with the warlock to the next
level. I texted him back.

You can't kill him.

I hit send and waited a few minutes. When I didn't get a
reply, I went inside. My new dad had apparently dropped
Mom off with Krista, who'd also found her way back to the
house, before he left for work again.

I scanned the living room, checking for any unwanted
warlocks lurking about, then went into the kitchen, a bright
thing with white cabinets and sparkling new appliances. Mom
sat at a small breakfast table and pointed to the coffee pot.

I raised my cup of motor oil and sat beside her. "Where's

Krista?"

"In her room."

"Oh, right," I said, infusing my voice with the bitterness I felt. "She has her own room."

"Annette, you really need to try to get along with your cousin. She's going through a tough time, and she's not the monster you make her out to be."

"Right. I'll work on that," I lied. "So, Mom, I don't mean to pry, but how can you afford this house?"

She blinked back at me. "Oh, Brad won a settlement. We paid cash for this baby."

While warning bells rang in my head so loud, I thought I was actually stuck inside one of them, Mom's gaze traveled lovingly over the space. A settlement. Was that how he got his spiffy new truck, too? Apparently, decent clothes were not a priority.

"How long have you known him?" I asked her.

"Brad?" She laughed like a schoolgirl. "Only a few months. I know it seems a little early to move in together, but Brad can be very persuasive."

I bet. Her eyes watered, and I realized how lonely she'd been. I'd always dreamed of her and my dad getting back together, but I guess that just wasn't meant to be. I leaned closer to her, just realizing she was wearing makeup. She hadn't been wearing makeup when I'd showed up on her doorstep, but she had been wearing it in the car, and the truth sank in.

"Mom, when I told you to get dressed so you could escape the warlock in the house, did you put on makeup?"

She patted her blushed cheeks. "Just mascara and blush." When I tossed her a dubious frown, she added, "And lipstick, but really, Annie. What does that have to do with anything?"

"You stopped to put on makeup with a warlock in the house?"

"It's not like it was on fire."

"The house or the warlock?"

Krista yelled out to me from her room, I assumed, her voice sounding like fresh acrylics on a chalkboard. "I need to talk to you!"

While she didn't say my name, we both knew who she meant. Mom offered me a sad smile and patted my hand. "Be nice to her."

"Sure thing."

Nice. I could do nice. I was often nice growing up. Not to her, but still. In my defense, she was mean to me first. I'd always idolized her, but a person could only take being bullied so long before the shine wore off and the true image broke through. Also, again, she put toothpaste in my hair. My recalcitrant curls were difficult enough to deal with. Toothpaste did not help, especially on a camping trip with only freezing-cold river water to wash it with.

I tended to hold on to grudges for dear life.

"Where are you?" I called out after having opened three hallway doors to no avail.

"In my room."

Resisting the urge to roll my eyes, I found her after the fourth try. She was folding laundry and stuffing it into a suitcase.

"Going back to hell so soon?" I asked.

Her jaw muscles bounced in response, letting me know I'd hit a nerve. Mission accomplished. "I'll have you know, I'm going to Mexico for a couple of weeks."

"Running from the law again?"

Her head snapped around so fast, her neck audibly cracked. For a minute I thought she broke it, then I remembered the possessed can do things like that without any permanent damage. I saw it in a movie once.

"Just kidding, cuz. What's the occasion?"

"I need to get away for a few days," she said, her voice shrill. Kind of like mine when in bird form. "Is that asking too much?"

"Sorry I asked."

I glanced out of her window, which faced the street, and watched little Apple ride her tricycle toward her grandmother's house again. How many times had she done that over the last few days? I suddenly wondered if Deph and I could do more. Could we help her move on? Help her go into the light, so to speak? I'd have to ask.

"What are you looking at?"

I turned back to my favorite—and only—cousin. "What do you want, Krista?"

She leaned over her bed, picked up her phone, and tossed it to me.

It was the wrong thing to do. She should have given me a heads-up, or shouted something like, "Think fast!" Instead, I swatted the device away like a wasp and it crashed into the wall. In my defense, she could've been throwing a snake at me. Or an artichoke. I hate artichokes.

"Was that new?" I asked.

She crossed her arms and faced me. "It was until it got fried by whatever thing you brought into this house."

"I thought you didn't believe in such things."

She did a sassy bob with her head. It wasn't a good look for her. "How else do you explain it, then? I had a brand-new phone go up in smoke. I tried to record you so I could finally go viral—"

Life goals.

"—and this happens." She stepped closer, towering over me. "Everything goes to shit when you're around. Why did you even come back?"

I'd had enough of being bullied for one day, so I stepped closer, too, forcing her back until the bed stopped her retreat.

But I had to admit, she had a point. Maybe it wasn't the warlock. Maybe I'd really fried her phone when she tried to record me. I'd certainly done worse in the last couple of weeks.

But Krista's behavior was a bit too caustic, even for her. Was something else going on?

"What do you want, Krista?"

She sat on the bed and pointed to the phone. "I want a new phone."

I gave her some space and leaned against her dresser, which looked brand new as well. The whole place reeked of newness. "And you want me to buy it?"

After tilting her head playfully, she said, "It's like the antique store. You break it, you buy it."

"Okay, but I only have three dollars in the bank. It'll take me a while to scrape the funds together."

Her jaw dropped. "How did you get here, then?"

"Credit card."

"Then use that."

"Maxed it out getting here," I lied. "Look, your phone malfunctioned. Just take it back."

"I can't!" she said, jumping to her feet. "I mean, I didn't get the insurance."

"But it was clearly faulty. Just take it back, insurance or no insurance."

Her face turned a bright shade of pink, and I knew that was my cue to get the heck out of Dodge. I turned toward the door, but a reflection in the mirror caught my attention. I squinted to make out what I was seeing. A bag sat on the closet floor, half opened with a pile of cash inside.

I caught Krista's gaze in the mirror, hers just as stunned as mine.

"Where did that come from?" And why was she asking me for money to buy a new phone when clearly she had plenty of the stuff?

"I wish you hadn't seen that." She picked up a cheer-leading trophy, which, what the fuck? She was only staying here for a few days and she brought her trophies? When she raised it over her head, I realized my cousin was planning to kill me right then and there. Again, what the fuck?

But instead of blind panic like I thought I'd feel when my ultimate demise loomed so very, very nigh, a calmness took over. A calmness like I'd never felt before. It filled my heart, fueled my lungs, and nourished my body as I looked up at my cousin with new eyes. As I saw the darkness poisoning her heart and soul.

She brought her hand down, the movement lightning quick, but it stopped in midair. Her expression morphed into one of pure shock a microsecond before it turned to cold, hard alabaster. She put up her other hand to stop me and reared back as though trying to take a breath, but she froze. Staring at me. Her arm ready to strike. Her other one trying to push me away. Her mouth open with the panic I should've felt. Like the rest of her, the summery blouse and capris she wore hardened to stone. Even the trophy she'd planned to kill me with turned to alabaster before my eyes.

I looked down and realized I'd touched her stomach. Just barely. Two fingertips. Just enough to... turn her to stone?

Gasping, I threw both hands over my mouth and stumbled back against the dresser.

My mom called out to us. "Is everything okay in there?"

I pressed my hands tighter over my mouth and squeezed my eyes shut. The room spun, and I felt the world tilt underneath my feet. I'd done it up good this time. How was I going to explain this? Better yet, how was I going to undo this? Betterer yet, how was I going to undo this without my cousin turning me in for attempted murder? If she was still alive, that is. Wait, was she? Did I kill her?

Barely able to breathe, I stepped closer to look at my

cousin's smooth face, long hair, pretty fingers. All stone now. All a beautiful pale alabaster. She'd always wanted better skin, so that was a plus, but her expression... It was like if Michelangelo had been hired to sculpt a horror movie set.

"Honey?" Mom said. I could hear her feet padding along the carpeted hallway.

When I finally managed to pry my hands off my mouth, I said, "It's all good, Mom. We're just chatting. You know, being nice."

"Okay. I called in to work. I think I'm going to lie down for a while."

"That's a great idea," I said just as I spotted the warlock in the mirror.

I swirled around to him.

As usual, he stood leaning against a wall, arms over his chest. But he no longer wore the coat, so his biceps bulged, testing the strength of the T-shirt he wore so exquisitely. Despite his chosen profession, I was glad to see him.

He looked at Krista, back at me, then at Krista again.

"I know, I know," I whispered, the sound like a radiator leak in the quiet room. "What do I do? Is she still alive? Can I bring her back?"

My phone dinged in my pocket. I took it out. It was him. Naturally.

When I kill people, I never worry about bringing them back. Not my strong suit.

Great. I glared at him. He shrugged a brow, and my phone dinged again. I looked down. It was him again. How did he text with his mind? I had to learn how to do that.

And glaring is not your strong suit, so give it up, buttercup.

"How are you texting me?"

Before I even finished asking the question, another text popped onto the screen. *Magic.*

Well, he was no use whatsoever. I eased closer to my cousin

and patted her face. No idea why. "Don't you worry, Krista. I'll figure this out. I'll turn you back. If it helps any, I was a bird for almost an entire day once."

The warlock visibly laughed. At least someone could.

I paced the room as the warlock looked on, his gaze part kid in a candy store and part predator. I stopped when another thought hit me and turned to him. "You didn't kill Brad, did you?"

He shook his head.

"Thank the goddess. That's all I need."

My phone dinged, only this time it wasn't the warlock. Speaking of whom, I really needed to learn his name if he was going to follow me around like this. At least when I got back to Salem, he wouldn't be able to enter the house. Percy was locked up tight against supernatural elements like him, corporeal or otherwise.

The text was from Defiance, a simple plea to call her.

I immediately tapped her info and pressed call. "Did you find her?" I asked when she picked up.

"I did. She's not dead, but she will be soon. You need to get there now."

Elation soared within me until confusion set in. "But I saw her."

"You saw her spirit. Her body is still alive, and you can save her."

I sank onto the bed. "Deph, I don't want to be a hero. Just tell me where she is and I'll call it in."

"Right, because they'll jump right on it. Do you know how many tips are called in with these things?"

Why was I hesitating? A child's life depended on me. I could save her, but I'd already destroyed one person today. What if I was too late? What if she died before I got there?

A text popped onto the screen. *Go.*

I looked at him. "What if I fail?"

"You won't," Deph said, but his expression softened.

I'll go with you.

For some bizarre reason, that thought gave me tremendous comfort.

I nodded. "Okay, I'll take my mom's car. She's lying down."

"Nette, hurry," Deph warned. Apparently, the situation was dire.

We hung up, but that left the dilemma of what to do with my cousin.

The warlock pointed to the bed.

"Put her in bed?" I asked. "She has to weigh a ton." Which was a sentiment she'd often conveyed to me over the years. One of Krista's favorite torments. My weight.

He shook his head and my phone dinged. *The blanket.*

"Oh, yeah, because a statue covered in a blanket in the middle of my cousin's bedroom won't be strange at all."

He fairly growled at me, only with his expression. *Deal with it later.*

I rolled my eyes, took the purple bedspread off the bed, and draped it over her. Not an easy task as she was way taller than me without the pointy trophy. It hit me again that my cousin was going to kill me. For money? Was I really worth so little to her?

After I got the cuz tucked in—she always looked good in purple—I sprinted toward the kitchen, grabbed my bag and Mom's keys, and booked it out of there. I stopped short when I saw Apple riding her tricycle again, pedaling like a duckling. Hopefully, she'd get to do that for real very soon.

My phone dinged. *Look.*

I glanced down the street in the opposite direction. A massive red truck was barreling its way toward us.

Chapter Five

"You are what you eat."
TF? When did I eat anxiety and back problems?
—Meme

I squeaked at the sight of Brad racing back to the house and hurried into my mother's crossover. I pulled out seconds before he screeched to a halt in front of the drive as though he was going to block me in.

He jumped out of the truck, every muscle in his body angry, but I didn't give him time to walk to the car. I floored it and watched him in the rearview, hands on his hips, an expression on his face that only a mother could love. He clearly wanted to stop me from leaving. Or, well, taking my mother's car. He'd made it abundantly clear he wanted me gone.

I followed Deph's directions. Actually, hers and Gigi's, as they argued over which route would be fastest. Deph's powers didn't come with actual GPS coordinates, but to say she could find a needle in a haystack would be quite the understatement. She was guiding me based on a map she'd printed of the area off the internet.

"It's some kind of landfill," Deph said, her tone filled with regret at even having to say something so terrible out loud. I could hear it in every syllable she spoke.

"This sucks," I said, making yet another left. At this rate, I was going to end up where I started.

"I know, hon, but you can do this."

I nodded and tried, for the ten thousandth time, not to look at the warlock in the passenger's seat. Even incorporeal, he filled the space with a presence that harkened back to royalty, his stoic confidence startlingly alluring. He pointed to a sign.

"We're almost there. We just passed a sign to the landfill."

"Who's with you?"

"I mean, me. *I'm* almost there."

"It's probably regulated," a man said, and I realized Salem's police chief and Gigi's fiancé, Houston Metcalf, had joined the effort.

"Hey, Chief," I said.

"Hey, you. How are you holding up?"

"Great. Wonderful. I'm terrified. I don't think I can do this."

"You'll be fine, hon. You may have to either sneak into the pit area or somehow convince the employees you have a good reason for combing through the landfill. Did you bring protective gear?"

"Protective gear?" I asked, hyperventilation becoming a real danger. "I'm still wearing my travel clothes, which are neither protective nor gear-like." The closer we got to the entrance, the more aggressive the butterflies in my stomach grew. Little assholes.

"It's okay. You should be fine, but if you have a mask, wear it."

"I do. I will." I took a right, at last, into the dump grounds of a small community on the outskirts of Phoenix.

"Deph, if she is here, she's been buried for days, baking in the Arizona heat underneath tons of garbage."

"She's still alive, babe. I can feel her heartbeat. It's faint, but she's a fighter."

I smiled at that knowledge.

"I called the local sheriff," the chief said. "He's going to meet you there."

"What did you tell him?" I asked as I turned toward the dumping area where cars could pull up and toss their rubbish over the side of a short but terrifying cliff.

"I told him you're a psychic who's helped me solve several cases."

"And he believed you?" I squeaked.

"No, but he's willing to give it a go."

The warlock gestured toward a parking area.

"I see it, but how do I get down to the actual dump?"

"You see what, hon?" Deph asked as the warlock pointed to a set of metal stairs. They were blocked off with a metal gate. I wasn't the best at jumping over barriers. This was just going to be sad.

"The parking area. I'm here and I don't see any workers, but there's a bulldozer running below."

"You have to stop it," Deph said.

I did. I knew it. And annoying people was kind of my area of expertise. "I've got this. If I can get down there."

"You go, girl," Gigi said, and I might have giggled if I hadn't been scared out of my mind.

I walked past a moving truck dumping garbage over the side of the cliff. Was that even safe? Signs covered the area. Apparently I was supposed to go to an office and pay to dump there, but I headed for the locked gate instead. After looking around for my shadow and not finding him, I stepped onto the bottom rung of the white metal gate and hefted a leg over it. It was a short leg and a tall gate, so my progress was slow. But when I saw a worker hurrying toward me, a man in coveralls and a bright orange baseball cap, a burst of adrenaline surged through me, and I dove headfirst over the metal barrier.

"Hey!" the man yelled as I landed shoulder first onto a panel of metal grating.

"It's okay!" I yelled back, struggling to my feet. "The sheriff is meeting me here."

I turned to see the warlock admiring my backside and almost gasped. He stood leaning against the railing, arms crossed over his chest as usual, head tilted to the side for a better angle. I swiped dirt off my ass and frowned at him.

He sobered and nodded to the stairs.

Without waiting for permission, I hurried down the steps.

"Hey, you can't go down there," the man said.

"It's okay!" I repeated. "The sheriff is meeting me here." I hurried to the pit and found a narrow walkway that led to the bulldozer, but even with a pathway, the journey was treacherous.

I waved my arms to stop him.

The driver stopped, ripped his mask down, and glared at me. He stepped out of the cab and yelled, "Are you crazy? What the hell are you doing?"

I'd been called worse. That very day, actually. "You have to stop!" I yelled over the motor. "The sheriff is coming!"

He tossed his hands into the air and shook his head before climbing back into the cab and cutting the motor.

That was so much easier than I'd thought it would be. I gave him a thumbs-up. He offered me another choice of fingers, but that was okay, too. I turned back to see the man coming up behind me, breathless and annoyed.

"You can't be out here," he said.

I was still on the call with Deph when my phone vibrated. I looked down.

Want me to take him out?

Without answering, because then I'd really look crazy, I just glared at the warlock who was now sitting on top of a pile of trash as though he were playing King of the Mountain. He had one leg drawn up and an arm balanced on it, the grin he wore infectious.

I shook my head then turned back to the worker. "Look," I said, realizing just how out of breath I was, "the sheriff got a tip. The missing girl, Apple James, is buried somewhere in here."

That startled him. He looked around as though he'd find her with one glance. If only it were that easy.

He pulled down his mask, one of those post-apocalyptic things with filters on either side, and pulled out his radio. "Hey, stop the dumpers. We need to conduct a search."

"Ten-four," the dispatch said.

"Is he bringing a dog? Because finding her will be almost impossible."

"Maybe." I put my hands on my hips and commiserated over the mountains of trash around me. Everything from recliners to exercise bikes filled the area.

"Wait," I said, looking at my phone for the exact date. "Five days ago. It would most likely have been five days ago. Is there a more likely place to look?"

"Yes." He pointed to my right. "We've been dumping mostly in section three for the last week. If she's here, she'd likely be there."

"Then that's where I'll start."

"By yourself?" he asked. "Dressed like that?"

I was wearing a light sweater, jeans, and sneakers. I didn't have anything any more appropriate than this. "Dressed like this," I affirmed.

"Then take this." He pulled the mask over his head and handed it to me. "And these." He peeled off his gloves and gave them to me.

"Thanks," I said, tugging the gloves on. "Any tips on how to get over all of this?"

"Carefully," he said. "I'll go wait for the sheriff."

I nodded and started toward the target area, my hopes falling more and more with each hazardous step I took. There was so much rubble. So much waste. How would I ever find her?

"Any idea where to look?" I asked into the phone, but I'd glanced up at the warlock, too, hoping for some hint. He had powerful magics, after all. Surely, he could do something to aid me in my search, but he shook his head.

"I don't know, Nette," Deph said. "I feel like you're close, I just can't pinpoint her location, she's so weak, and I feel like something is blocking me."

"The warlock?" I asked. "Could he be blocking you?"

"Wait, is he there, Annette?" Gigi asked.

"Yes," I said. "He's been helping me."

My sleuthing partners went silent, but I didn't have time to listen to all the reasons I was making a mistake. No matter his reason, the warlock had been helping. Enemies with a common goal, so to speak.

I stumbled over the small mountain, the bottom layers of which had been steamrolled flat. It was the layers on top that were difficult to navigate. Thanking the goddess for the gloves and mask, even though the latter blocked my vision a little, I looked back at the warlock, but he was gone. Executing a classic three-sixty, I found him on top of another mountain, scouring the area.

"This is hopeless," I said to no one in particular.

"Nette, you need to use your powers," Defiance said.

"Right. I don't think that's a good idea."

"You saved Roane's life," she argued, talking about her boyfriend. The kilted one who occasionally turned into a wolf. "You're capable of so much more than you know, but it seems like it takes extreme circumstances to focus our energies."

"You got that right," I said, thinking of my poor cousin.

"Now is the time, love," the chief said.

"No pressure." I stood straight and started to concentrate on my powers—whatever that entailed—when a soft voice drifted toward me.

"What are you doing here?" she asked.

I looked up and saw Apple watching me from the top of the cliff, which didn't look as tall from this angle. "I'm trying to save your little ass."

Her tiny brows slid together, and she put her chin on her handlebars. "He's going to be mad."

My lungs froze. "He?"

"The man who hit me. He rolled me up in a rug and threw me down here."

After a moment of shocked silence, I snapped out of it. For her. "A rug?" I asked, scanning the area frantically. "Do you remember the color, baby?"

"Of course."

When she didn't elaborate, I looked up at her. "And?"

"And what?"

"What color was the rug he rolled you in?"

"Oh." She straightened in her seat and looked up in thought.

Hope had kickstarted my heart, quickly sending it into overdrive.

The warlock was feeling it too, his eyes on the girl as though breathless with anticipation.

"You saw it, right?" I asked.

56

"Yes, but I don't remember the word."

"The word?" I asked, growing more frustrated with each passing second. "Can you give me something close?"

She literally tapped her finger on her little chin. "Well, it's green but also blue."

I spun around, looking for that color. "Green but also blue. Teal, maybe? Turquoise?"

"That's it!" She clapped her hands. "Grandma Lou calls it turquoise."

"Turquoise. A turquoise rug. A turquoise rug." I whirled around in circles.

"But that's the inside of the rug."

I spun back to her. "The inside?"

"Yes, that's what I could see. I don't know what color the outside is."

Damn it. She had a point. The backing of the rug could very well be a different color.

She put her chin on the handlebars again, her lids drifting slowly shut.

"Annette," Deph said through the speaker, "I'm losing her."

"She's trying to go to sleep," I said, fighting the fear rising in my throat. I looked over and saw the worker I'd spoken to walking toward us, the sheriff and a deputy close behind him.

"I'm losing her," Deph said. "There's some kind of block. I feel like she's had a spell cast over her to keep her safe, but it's blocking me."

"Maybe her parents are witches?" I suggested. "Or her grandmother?" Not that it mattered now.

"Annette," Gigi said, her voice doing the calm thing again, "you're a charmling, love. You should be able to feel her."

"I know. I should, but I can't. I don't feel anything. I'm not like Deph."

"It could be the same thing blocking me," Deph said.

I once saw her find a ring buried in the ground decades earlier, pinpointing its exact location with utter ease. "If it's blocking you, Deph, I don't stand a chance. Wait a minute," I said when realization dawned. "I'm a carrion."

"You're a what?" Deph asked.

I looked over at the warlock. His mouth slid into a knowing smile.

"I'm a carrion."

"Like the luggage?" Gigi asked.

"No," I said, laughing. "Not a carry-on." I looked for a place to hide and quickly found a drop-off to my left. It was perfect since the men were coming up on my right. I looked up at the warlock and said, "Wish me luck."

He shook his head, refusing. The jerk.

After one more glance at Apple, her antennae tilting to the side as she drifted into oblivion, I ran to the edge of the trash pile and jumped down the side, focusing with all of the concentration my ADHD-riddled brain could muster.

I shifted before my feet hit the ground, which was good. I was not a spring chicken.

Laughing at my own joke, I flew up past the men who tried to see where I went, my black wings spread wide and flapping to gain altitude. Hopefully that would shock the men enough to keep them from looking over the side and finding my clothes.

"Annette?" Deph said, but no way was I speaking to her. I could, but my voice was ridiculous, and it would definitely freak out the men wading through the trash pile.

But it worked. Despite the filth and rotting trash, the poor baby girl's scent drifted toward me. It both saddened and exhilarated me. I circled close by as the men cupped their hands over their eyes to watch me, but we were on the wrong pile. I landed on a hill close by and pecked at the top layers, moving plastic bottles and torn garbage bags until I made a small opening. Until I saw her antennae poking out at me.

Relief filled every molecule in my body. Now to shift and get dressed without the men spotting me, but the odds of that were slim since they were all three now looking over the edge, having seen my clothes. I had no choice but to shift behind them.

Ignoring the fact that the warlock could see everything, I aimed at the men's backs and drifted toward them, shifting seconds before landing. The sound of me landing was enough to get the deputy's attention. He turned, but I lifted my hand and drew a spell on the air. Neon green burst from the symbol I drew, the neon light bleeding through the lines I'd drawn.

It was a simple spell. An invisibility spell. Because I was naked in front of several men, and while I did consider stripping in college once for a little extra spending money, being naked in front of a landfill full of men was not my idea of a good time.

I only prayed the spell worked on the warlock as well. Judging by the expression on his face as he knelt on the top of his mountain, balancing on the balls of his feet, his head tilted to the side again for a better view, I hazarded a guess and said no. Not aloud. The spell was for invisibility. It had nothing to do with sound.

Or touch, as I found out when I tried to hurry past them to my clothes. I brushed against the worker as I navigated the filth barefooted and quickly found myself in his grip. His hand caught my wrist, and he looked as surprised as I felt.

Before I could react, the man went sailing back. He landed several feet away.

I refocused on the warlock, the anger on his face apparent.

He offered me a quick nod and then vanished. I did a one-eighty but gave up quickly. I had to get to Apple.

After half sliding down the edge of the hill, making a note

to get a tetanus shot ASAP, I hurried into my clothes then canceled the spell with a swipe of my hand.

"I found her!" I shouted to the men.

They were still trying to figure out what happened to the worker but hurried over to help me up the man-made structure. The sheriff and deputy caught my hands and pulled me up over the edge.

The worker seemed no worse for the wear, so I rushed to the next hill and found the spot I'd cleared. "She's here."

"You found her?" Deph asked in unison with the sheriff.

"I did." Together we dug through the rubble and pulled the rug out as I watched Apple on her trike. "Apple!" I yelled, pretending to be yelling at the girl in the carpet, but I was trying to get the girl on the trike's attention.

It worked. She blinked sleepily and looked over at us.

"How fast can you get an ambulance here?" I asked the sheriff.

"Pretty damned," he said.

Normally, they would never mess with a crime scene, but I assured them she was still alive. I could feel her heartbeat with my psychic powers. They didn't buy it but went along with it anyway. We carefully put the rug on the top of the mountain and rolled it open with painstaking slowness. A little girl covered in filth and blood appeared. Some of her skin was stuck to the rug, and my brain couldn't even process the insects crawling all over her.

The deputy knocked them off as the sheriff checked for signs of life. It took only seconds before he was on his radio calling for a helicopter.

I was more grateful than he would ever know. An ambulance would take too long.

"Ten minutes," he said. Then he took his bottled water, poured some into his hands, and patted it over her face, neck, and bare arms, trying to cool her down while the deputy used the water to unstick her limbs from the fabric.

"Oh," Apple said beside me, perking up. "You found me."

I smiled over at her, took the phone off speaker, and walked a few feet away, pretending to talk into it. I knelt down to her. "We did it. We found you, pumpkin."

Sirens sounded in the distance, and she turned toward them, saying almost absently, "He's going to be mad."

"Why is that?"

"Because he said he had a plan and he couldn't let a little brat riding a bike in the middle of the street in the middle of the night mess it up for him."

He sounded like a great guy. The men were watching me, but I'd already claimed to be a psychic. Talking to the dead was kind of my job. "Do you know who it was, baby?"

She shook her head. "I only smelled cigarettes when he picked me up."

It took a moment for my mind to wrap around the implications of what she said. Tons of people still smoked, but there were simply too many coincidences to ignore. I closed my eyes when all the pieces fell into place. "Sweetheart, were you going to your grandmother's house?"

She nodded, but before she could say anything, she vanished. I hurried to her side as a soft moan escaped her throat. The men high-fived each other, their faces lighting up with elation when they looked up at the helicopter hovering overhead.

"We need to wait for a stretcher," the sheriff said.

"Okay." I fought back tears, the adrenaline rush intoxicating as I spotted another piece of the puzzle in my periphery. I pointed to her trike. The same trike that had somehow made it into the spiritual realm with Apple. "That's her tricycle, by the way."

The sheriff turned and nodded. "We'll have forensics process it and take it in."

Two first responders in hospital masks and black uniforms hurried toward us, the male carrying a bright orange stretcher, the female a medical kit. She was pretty, her bronze hair pulled back into a bun at the nape of her neck, showing off her clear, dark skin.

We moved back to let them work. The man called in her vitals. The woman wasted no time in starting an IV. But Apple wasn't out of the woods yet. She'd made it this far, fought so hard to stay alive, yet she'd been in the heat too long. If nothing else, there could be extensive brain damage.

I had to question my purpose again. Why me? Why was I a charmling? An alchemist? A healer? And who needed healing more in this moment than this little girl?

While the EMTs worked, I stepped closer. Unless someone here was a witch or was burdened with a mental illness, no one but me would be able to see the light spilling out of a spell if I performed one.

I'd practiced several healing spells, but to really put one to work required a skill level I had yet to achieve. I'd healed Deph's boyfriend, but that was so random. It just came out of nowhere. Could I do something like that again? I had no choice but to try. Still, a little confidence would've been nice.

I closed my eyes and sought the spell I needed in the vastness of the magics I had inside me. Apparently, they came with the gig. I rushed past this spell and that, looking for the exact symbol to draw on the air when I almost missed it. I stopped, reached out, and took it into my hand.

Bringing it forward into this world, I drew the spell as nonchalantly as I could manage on the air above Apple. Light burst from the lines, and a brilliant green flooded the area. Apple cracked open her eyes to look at it. She barely caught a glimpse of the light before it sank into her, flooding her body with magics to heal body and mind. Spirit would be up to her. The trauma would always be there, but I had a feeling, with the proper help, she could handle it.

Apple moaned softly again as the warmth of the spell soaked into her, and the sweetest smile widened across her face.

"That's it, baby," the female EMT said as she secured a brace around her neck. "This is a walk in the park. You're going to be just fine."

I took that as my cue to leave, after looking around for the warlock, to no avail. How could I be surprised? I'd fulfilled my purpose. I'd found the girl like he wanted, but a goodbye would've been nice. Still, the thought of being enslaved for all eternity convinced me to leave it alone.

As another set of first responders descended the stairs, I hurried past them. The sheriff and his deputy could take all the credit. The last thing I needed was for the news to get a hold of my name.

"Chief?" I said into the phone, not sure he would still be there.

"I'm here, sweetheart. You did good."

The three of them clapped and cheered into the phone.

"Thanks to you guys. I know she's not out of the woods, but at least we gave her a fighting chance. And I know who hit her."

"Who?" Deph asked.

"I'm about ninety percent certain it was my mom's new boyfriend, Brad, but I don't know his last name. I'll find out and get that info to you if you wouldn't mind calling it in to the sheriff, Chief."

"I can do that."

"And can you check in with him? Let me know how Apple is doing?"

"I can do that, too."

"Thank you."

"Be careful, Annette," Deph said.

"I will. I have a few things to tie up, then I'll head back."

Two questions loomed over my head like a dark cloud. First, how would I get my mother away from a possible child killer and, if my instincts were correct, a con man? And second, what on the great goddess's earth was I going to do with my cousin?

Chapter Six

"*Do what you love and money will follow.*"
Ate pizza. Drank wine. Took a five-hour nap.
Now I wait.
—Meme

I drove back to the house in silence, mostly because I was alone. The warlock wasn't with me. Not that isolation ever kept me from talking to myself, but I just wasn't in the mood for my shit right now. It had been a busy day, and it was barely five in the afternoon. I still had hours to go before bedtime, yet I wanted nothing more than a hot drink, a cool shower, and a soft bed. Oh, and a surefire way to hide a statue from my mother while keeping her away from the new man in her life.

My mother had to come first. Krista wasn't going anywhere. My priority would have to be getting Brad away from her for good, which meant proving he'd not only driven the truck that ran over Apple, but that he dumped her body as well. Intent. That was the key to locking him up for a long time. I silently thanked Investigation Discovery for my education in criminal investigation. Goddess, I learned a lot from that channel. Including how to gather evidence. I hadn't seen any cameras at the landfill, but I wasn't looking for any at the time either. And surely we could get other camera footage that would have been along his path.

When I got back to the house, Mom was asleep. "Mom?" I said, sneaking into her room. The curtains had been drawn, blocking much of the sunlight from entering. If there was one thing Arizona had an abundance of, it was sunshine.

She turned over in her bed to face me and said sleepily, "Hey, honey. Where have you been?"

"I had an errand to run. Sorry I took your car without asking."

"Brad was pretty upset."

"I'm sure he was. Where is he?"

She scooted up to rest against the headboard and spared a moment to take me in, only making me a little uncomfortable. It was strange to be in my forties and still worry about what my mother thought of me. One side of her short brown hair had been squashed, and she wore a short-sleeve peasant gown with colorful stitching along the neckline, and the image was kind of adorable. I'd never in all my years thought of my mother as adorable, but there ya go.

She seemed tired, however, and it was probably my fault. She'd had to deal with Brad when I stole her car and went for a joyride. At least, I was certain that's what he thought.

"Are you like him?" she asked almost forlornly, and for some reason I knew exactly who she was talking about.

I chewed on my bottom lip in thought, trying to figure out how to answer her, and then shook my head. "No, I'm not. But I do come from him. From his blood."

"So, he's a part of you."

"No matter what I do, yes, he is."

She nodded, absorbing the information. "Will you become like him?"

"To become like him, I'd have to practice the black arts, and I have no intention of doing that."

"That's what everyone thought about Willow, and look what happened to her."

I blinked in surprise. My mother just referenced *Buffy the Vampire Slayer*. I couldn't have been more shocked if she'd hauled off and slapped me. "You're a Buffy fan?"

"Duh," she said.

Again, a shockwave rocketed through my core, shaking my brain. Who was this woman?

"Well," she said as though changing her mind, "I guess you could say I'm more of a Spike fan, but apples and oranges and all."

"Spike, huh? I figured you for more of an Angel fan." Like me, because damn. There was nothing sexier than a tall gorgeous man who could wear clothes that well.

"I was at first," she said, "but then Spike showed up and I lost all sense of morality."

"Yeah, that happened to a lot of people when Spike showed up." I laughed but cut it short when I saw a dark figure—*the* dark figure—standing in the corner of her room. A tiny thrill laced up my spine. Talk about tall gorgeous men who wore clothes well.

I didn't tell Mom. No need to send her into a frenzy after this morning.

"Are all warlocks bad?" she asked me.

I glanced over at him, and he raised a single brow, clearly very interested in my answer.

Ignoring the rush of heat that gesture sparked inside me, I lifted a noncommittal shoulder. I'd actually heard there were warlocks who weren't completely evil. They practiced the black arts, but they didn't use them to hurt or take advantage of others. Maybe Tall, Dark, and Deadly was like that. Not so much evil as... experimental. Like grunge bands back in the day before they became a thing.

"I'm not really sure," I said to her. "I've heard there are a few that practice the black arts for honorable reasons. I just don't know what those could be. Again, I'm pretty new to all of this."

She nodded and glanced to the side as though looking out the window.

I took the opportunity to catch a quick glimpse of the warlock, wondering why he was here if I'd already accomplished what he'd asked. Did he need something else from me? Was that how it started? The enslavement?

Of course, any warlock worth his weight would never try to keep a blood heir all to himself. Apparently, charmlings are impossible to control completely. We're simply too powerful. So he would have to transfer my powers to another witch. A female witch, since males could not assume our powers. A female witch he could control, and the blood heir—aka, *moi* —would die in the process.

Perhaps that was his ultimate goal. His master plan to lure me into complacency and then roofie me so he could perform the ceremony to steal my powers. If so, he was doing a bang-up job of it.

"I was scared of you," Mom said in a small voice, still pretending to look out the window.

"What?"

"When you were growing up, I was scared of who you could become. And then when Austin went missing—"

"Oh my God, Mom." I eased away from her. "Did you think that was me? That some dark part of me... what? Killed my own brother?"

"No," she said, leaning forward to take my hand and pull me back. "Not exactly."

"But it was there in the back of your mind," I said matter-of-factly.

She nodded. "I'm sorry."

"No, don't be. It explains a lot."

Her eyes drifted shut. "Again, I'm sorry. Your father and I didn't blame you. We really didn't. But..."

"There was a part of you that had to wonder." And how could I blame her for that? It was only natural after what she'd been through. After what I'd come from. It explained why I'd gotten that impression from my mother, too, and not my dad. "It's okay, Mom." Since we were being so open and honest, now was the perfect time to bring up her taste in men. I glanced at the warlock in the corner, and an old saying about the pot calling the kettle black came to mind, but I barreled forward regardless.

"Mom, we really need to talk about Brad."

She drew in a shaky breath and refocused on me. "Do you want to talk about how he's a schemer and a con artist, or the fact that he ran that sweet little girl over and left her for dead?"

Again, the shockwave that shot through me like a bullet left me speechless. Not for long, but still. "You knew?"

Her small shoulders rose in a hapless shrug. "I suspected. When I heard she used to live here and she spent most of her time at her grandmother's house next door, I began to wonder if she'd taken it upon herself to come for a visit."

"And that led to your suspicions?"

She examined her half-eaten nails for a moment, then said, "Well, that and the blood on Brad's clothes after he came home late one night."

My heart tripped on its own beat. Blood on his clothes? That there was what we armchair sleuths called evidence. I cleared my throat and asked as though almost uninterested in her answer, "And where are those clothes now?"

After a moment of staring off into space, she turned back

to me as though she'd lost her train of thought. Then she said sadly, "With the police."

It took a long while for me to comprehend what she'd just said. When it finally sank in, I asked, "You turned him in?"

"Of course, Annette. What do you take me for?"

"And you knew he was a con man?"

"Not at first, but there are red flags and then there are glowing scarlet banners the size of skyscrapers." She scootched her lips to one side of her face and explained, "He's the latter, by the way."

I grinned. "I figured. But why are you still here if you knew what kind of person he is?"

"Honey," she said, patting my hand as though I were a little slow on the uptake, "do you remember that time you got out of finals by pretending me and your father had gone missing and you hadn't seen us in a week and you were sure we got sucked up in the Bermuda Triangle?"

After a reminiscent laugh, I sobered and bowed my head apologetically. "Yes."

"And the fact that your teachers fell for it?"

"Yes. Sorry about that."

"Where do you think you get that skill from?"

"Wait, you're acting?" I tried not to gape at her. I failed. "You know what he is, the atrocious things he's done, and you've been going along with it? Why?"

"Because he is very good at what he does, and I think he's conned your cousin into something terrible."

The bag of money in her closet popped into my mind. "I think you're right, Mom."

"I've been working with the police for a couple of weeks now and, if all goes as planned, I'm going to say she has been in on it with me the whole time."

Of course she would do that. Krista didn't deserve my mother. And she tried to kill me. I decided to hate her, but only a little considering her current state. "You're pretty incredible," I said, the words foreign on my tongue. At least when it came to my mom. Why didn't we have this conversation years ago? Then again, would I have believed her? That she'd been roofied. That my biological father was a warlock? That I came from a long line of witches? Wait, maybe she didn't know that last part.

"Back atcha," she said, a capricious grin playing about her mouth.

I leaned forward and pulled her into a deep hug. The kind that heals wounds. The kind I'd dreamt of my whole life.

"Annie?" she said at my ear almost meekly.

"Yes?"

"I did have one more question."

I set her at arm's length. "Shoot."

She held up a finger. "First, I want you to know I'm not accusing you of anything."

Uh-oh. Lines like that always led to an accusation of some kind. "Okay," I said warily.

"And if the answer is yes, I will understand."

"Okay," I said even more warily.

"And it's not like I don't understand your life choices."

Holy crap, did she know about the warlock? "Mom, you're killing me. What is it you think I've done?"

She pursed her lips in determination and asked, "Did you happen to turn your cousin into a statue?"

Chapter Seven

Growing up is when you stop being scared of villains
and start wanting to have sex with them.
—Meme

I managed the hot drink and the cool shower. Now I just needed a soft bed. And not the one I was sitting on at that moment, either.

Mom and I sat on Krista's bed, staring up at my cousin as though we were in a museum, contemplating the meaning of our existence. Kind of. We were actually staring at the duct tape on Krista's finger. When I took the bedspread off her, I snagged it on her hand and broke off her pinkie. I could only hope it didn't hurt her if she was still in there. Just in case, we got some duct tape and reattached that baby. If I did manage to turn her back, she'd want all of her fingers. She was vain that way.

The warlock followed us. He lifted himself onto the dresser, the movement silent, and sat with a long arm thrown casually over one raised knee, and I could hardly take my eyes off the man. But I realized he was wearing a black button-down. Not the long designer coat. Nor the tee from earlier. Whatever he wore on his physical body must be what he wore in the veil. It traveled with him, much like Apple's clothes and tricycle.

"You have to take her back to Salem with you and figure out how to destone her," Mom said, drawing me back to her, aghast.

"How am I going to get her to Salem? She's really heavy now." I snickered. I loved saying that about her. Weight was always such a big deal to her, I prayed she could hear me from the great beyond. Or the mediocre here. Either way.

"Let me think." She began chewing on her nails again. I'd never noticed her do that. "Wait, what happened to the warlock?" She glanced around, wide-eyed. "Has he come back?"

"Nope," I lied. The second the word left my mouth, my phone dinged. The same phone I'd been carrying around for fear the chief would call me with an update and I might miss it. I'd called him, letting him know the police here were well aware of Brad's evil deeds and were on it. Hopefully the man would be arrested soon.

I read the text—*Liar, liar, pants on fire.*—and glared at him. First, how the hell did he text so fast? Second, what other things did he do fast?

"What about the money?" she asked, breaking into my thoughts yet again. "If Brad finds it, he'll run."

"Do you know how she got it? What he conned her into doing?" If he conned her at all. My mom may be a savvy goddess, but Krista had always been able to pull the faux wool over her eyes. For all I knew, it was Krista who wrangled Brad into her machinations.

"Unfortunately, I don't. That was one reason it took me

so long to go to the police. I was trying to figure out what those two were up to, what he was trying to convince her to do."

"Where is she working now?"

"At a bank."

I deadpanned her. "And you don't think that might be pertinent to our investigation?"

"Well, now that you mention it. You know what? I have a friend of a friend who might have an answer."

"That doesn't sound sketchy at all. With how my hair-brained cousin managed to pull off a bank job?"

"What? No. And we don't know that it was a bank job. Wouldn't it have been on the news?"

She had me there. "Then an answer to what?"

"How you can get your cousin to Salem." She changed subjects as quickly as I did. Now I knew where I got it from.

"Oh, right," I said, deflating. "I guess it has to be done."

"Did you break her finger off on purpose?"

I gasped for a solid thirty seconds, then said, "Maybe subconsciously. I'm not sure."

She leaned closer and whispered, "Did you turn her into a statue on purpose?"

"No," I said, shaking my head. "I never even knew I could do such a thing."

We turned and stared at her some more until another thought hit me. "Oh my God, I know what to do."

"Okay."

I surged to my feet and started walking in circles around my nemesis. "You're already talking to the police. How about we forge a note from her to you saying that she regrets everything she did. She wants you to turn the money over to the police while she goes away for a few weeks to get her head straight."

Mom stood and pointed at me. "That's not bad. Do you think you can figure out how to turn her back in a few weeks?"

"I have no idea, but with Deph's and Gigi's help, not to mention the entire coven, I'm sure we can come up with something."

"There's a coven?"

I smiled. "There's a coven. Okay, let's get the money."

Mom rushed to look out the window to make sure Brad wasn't home, then hurried to the walk-in closet to help me. "We can put it in the freezer for now. I'll write the note, then we can transfer the money to my car when Brad is at work tomorrow."

I'd bent to pick up the bag of money. She'd stuffed it into a blue sports duffle bag but left the zipper open so anyone walking into her room could see it. Krista wasn't the brightest, but she wasn't an idiot either. Leaving it open like that was a bit much. Then I noticed several more duffle bags, exactly like the first, scattered along the ground, only these were empty. One was stuck underneath one of the bare shelving units. She hadn't brought that many clothes with her. I went to pull it out, and the entire unit moved. That was when the shiny wallpaper behind the shelves grabbed my attention. I slid them out further. The wallpaper didn't match the rest of the house, so I looked closer and froze.

"Oh my God," Mom said, trying to pick up the heavy duffle. "This is so much money."

"Mom."

"What did she do, Annie? How could she ever get a hold of this much money?"

"Mom," I repeated.

Giving up on lifting the bag, she stood and raised her brows at me in question.

"This isn't bank money."

She stepped closer to see what I was looking at. "What do you mean?"

"This is drug money." I turned to her. "This is cartel money."

She squinted at the bales of twenties, at least a dozen, wrapped in plastic and stacked high behind the loose shelving unit. What the actual fuck?

I motioned for her to follow me. "We have to get out of here."

"What? Why?" She leaned into one of the bales. "Is that money?"

"There has to be millions of dollars here, Mom." I pushed the unit closed and tugged at her gown. "We have to go. Now."

"What did that girl get herself into?"

"I don't know and I don't want to find out." I turned to the warlock. "Did you know about this?"

He shrugged a shoulder like it was no biggie.

"Who are you talking to? Oh my God, is he here?"

Crap, I forgot. "He is, but it's okay, Mom. He helped me find Apple."

"He helped?" she asked, spinning in circles looking for him. "I thought he was a warlock."

"He is, but he's not my worry at the moment. We need to leave." Before we could get to her car I'd parked in the garage, however, we heard the sound of a motor revving up the drive.

We rushed to the window. Brad threw open his door and got out, his movements agitated as he slammed it shut behind him.

"He's here," Mom said. "And he's none too happy by the looks of him."

He'd opened the garage door and walked into the living room via the access door there.

Mom swallowed hard. "We just have to act nonchalant."

"Right. Nonchalant. I can do nonchalant." But could I do it knowing the man I was acting for was a cold-blooded killer? And a thief? And who knew what else? "Time to put that one semester of drama I had in college to good use."

She nodded, and we hurried out of Krista's room and into Mom's. She put on a robe, and we walked out to greet the man of the house.

The warlock was already there, holding up yet another wall. He had a tough job.

"Hey, you," Mom said, a warm smile on her face, and I found myself in awe of her. While I was fairly quaking in my boots, she was as calm as a summer breeze.

He tossed me a hard glare, then strode past us to his and Mom's bedroom. "I have to go out of town for a while," he said over his shoulder.

"Oh?" She followed him, and I fought the urge to grab onto the sleeve of her robe to keep her from doing so. "For work?"

"Yes."

I heard him rummaging through drawers.

The TV came on then, and a news story belted out the fact that Apple James had been found and was expected to make a full recovery.

I turned to the warlock. One corner of his mouth tilted heavenward.

Brad stormed out of the bedroom, looked at the TV, then at me, then back at the TV before turning it off by punching the power button with his fist, and a satisfaction like I'd never known before washed over me. She beat him. A five-year-old girl won, and he was not taking it well, but was that why he suddenly had to get out of town?

"Can you believe it, honey?" Mom asked him. "They found that sweet little girl."

He grunted and opened the door to Krista's room.

I held my breath. This was it. Would he go for all of the money? Would he just take a little now, then come back for more later?

"Why the fuck does Krista have a statue of herself in the middle of our guest room?"

"Does she?" Mom hurried over and peeked inside. "Good heavens, that is beautiful. It looks just like her."

He slammed the door shut, almost hitting my mom in the face.

I started forward, but the warlock appeared before me, blocking my path. Then again, could he? He was incorporeal. Couldn't I just walk through him? What could he do to stop me? Then I remembered the man who went flying when he took hold of my arm at the landfill.

"Where is she?" Brad asked, his tone razor sharp. "She was supposed to let me know before leaving the house."

"Why would she need to do that, honey?" Mom was good.

"Because she has something of mine."

Something like millions of dollars? Did he really not know it was only a few feet away from him? And, again, how the actual hell did my cousin, who'd barely graduated high school, get her hands on that kind of money? Was that really why the cuz was here? Was she hiding from someone and, in turn, brought that trouble to my mother's doorstep? How dare she put Mom in danger like that.

As I stared the warlock down, the blue glittering in his eyes enchanting me, Brad took out his phone to call her. "When I get my hands on that woman. A fucking statue of herself. Who the fuck gets a statue of themselves?" He tossed an article of clothing on the floor in the hall, and I hoped it wasn't underwear. Because ew.

"I think she fried her phone this morning," Mom said. "I believe she was going to go get a new one."

"Then why is her car in the driveway?" His tone toward my mother was so caustic, it scraped along my nerve endings.

My irritation with the man soared, but the warlock gazed at me from underneath his thick lashes and shook his head in warning.

"Is it? Maybe she went with some friends. You know how she is. What do you want for dinner?"

"I don't have time." He tossed me another glare for good measure and marched back into the bedroom to resume his packing.

Mom walked into the kitchen. "At least have some coffee before you go." She hurried to the coffee pot, and I watched her like she'd lost her mind. Let the man go, for goddess's sake. We had to get out of there ourselves before the cartel showed up and opened fire.

I walked to the kitchen, too, and shrugged at her in question.

She took her phone out of a pocket in the robe and showed it to me. *On the way*, it said, but it didn't identify the caller.

Hilariously, the warlock appeared behind me and peeked over my shoulder to see, too. He was so close to me, but I couldn't hear him. Or feel him. No breath. No warmth. I wanted to ease back until I would technically be touching him but didn't dare. Who knew what he could do? What he was capable of?

Mom leaned close to me and whispered, "My contact. They must have gotten enough evidence for an arrest, but if he leaves this house, he will disappear. I found several identities and a bug-out bag hidden in the toolbox of his truck."

"You broke into his toolbox?" I asked, more impressed than ever.

"No. A friend of mine did."

"You have some crazy friends, Mom."

"Well, you'll meet this one. He has the perfect car for you to take Krista to Salem with you."

"Nice. In the meantime, what do we do about my new dad?"

She snorted, and Brad stepped out of the bedroom, eyeing us suspiciously with a glare as sharp as shattered glass. "What are you two talking about?"

"Dinner," Mom said happily. "We're thinking Italian. Are you sure you can't stay?"

"I'm sure." He disappeared into the bedroom again.

"At least have some coffee before you go. I don't want you falling asleep on the road."

"Fine."

"We have to stall him."

"Mom, we have to get out of here. If the cops come and he's not in the mood to cooperate, this could quickly escalate into a hostage situation."

She nodded, her brows drawn tight in concern. "You're right."

My phone dinged. *Take him the coffee yourself.*

I glared at the man standing beside me. The impossibly tall one towering over me like a gothic castle. Either that or I'd read way too many romance novels. But he didn't know what he was asking of me. "You take him the coffee," I said to Mom.

She stilled when she realized the warlock was right behind us. She inched to her left, trying to get away from him as a sly, knowing smile spread across his face.

I stared at him for a solid minute. Did he know about my disastrous history of accidentally turning substances like salt and coffee into all manner of lethal concoctions?

My phone dinged, and it took me a moment to tear my gaze off of his. When I finally managed it, the text read, *Personally, I'd just dose him, but I suppose cyanide would get the job done just as well.*

My gaze darted back to his. He *did* know. How? How could he possibly—?

"Where's my new jeans?" Brad called out to Mom.

"Let me look in the dryer." She tossed me a worried expression, then hurried to the laundry room.

The warlock leaned against the counter where my mom had been standing and gestured toward the pot.

"I can't poison him," I said. "Mom will be questioned. Me, too."

Then dose him, he texted.

"It's not that easy," I whispered, but he only smiled, a small beautiful thing that flipped my stomach like a pancake. "Fine. Dose him. I can do this." I grabbed a pod and put it in the machine. After it brewed a rich dark coffee that had my mouth watering, I took the cup, wrapped both hands around it, and concentrated on the word *sedative*.

It appeared in my mouth like magic. Probably because it was magic. I leaned over the cup and blew softly, letting the magics flow out of me and into the aromatic elixir.

"Is that mine?" he asked, having appeared on the other side of the island.

I jumped, spilling some of the hot liquid on my hand. "It is. Do you take cream or sugar?"

He held out his hand without answering, his scruffy brows drawn sharply.

I handed the cup over and prayed he wouldn't drop dead. Not yet anyway.

"I thought you were leaving," he said before he took a sip and sat at the table to trim his nails while I tried not to gag.

"Found 'em," Mom said. "Do you want to shower before you go?"

"No time." He took another long draught of coffee and I almost fainted. If there was even a trace of cyanide in it like the last time I tried to hand someone a cup of coffee, oblivious at the time that I had inherited magics, he would not survive the dose.

He looked back at me, clearly wondering why I was staring at him. I was rusty at the whole acting thing. I'd forgotten how to do nonchalance while my mother was a pro.

"Okay," she said, coming out of the bedroom. "I put them in your duffle bag along with some extra underwear."

He looked up at her. "Where are you going?"

She'd changed out of her robe and flung her bag over her shoulder. "I told you," she said, her voice as light as air. "Italian. Though I really think you should come with us. Get a bite before you go." She refocused on me. "You ready?"

I was almost afraid to leave him in the house alone. If he found that money. . .

He won't find it, he texted. *Go.*

Glancing at the warlock, I didn't ask how he was planning on stopping Brad if he decided to search Krista's room.

"Did you dose him?" Mom asked.

I looked over, and Brad had fallen asleep in the fingernail castoffs. "It worked."

"How did you do that?"

"Magic," I said, pleased with myself until reality sank in and panic almost closed my throat. "Wait, is he dead?"

Mom giggled and lifted his eyelid. "Nope. Just sleeping." She looked at me. "You really did that?"

"I really did that," I said with a sigh of relief. "He's not foaming at the mouth or anything?"

"No. Okay, now what?"

Without thinking, I turned to the warlock.

He didn't take his eyes off me, but my phone dinged. He could text without looking. So jelly. *Go. Or I'll make you go.*

Ballsy. "Do you know how Krista got that money?"

He nodded.

"Tell me," I said, anticipation rising inside me.

82

Her husband is a courier for the cartel. He brings semi-trucks full of cash into the country to launder.

I didn't want to know how he knew that. "Mom," I said, showing her the text.

Mom gaped at me. "Is he... is he texting you?"

I nodded. "Did you know this?"

She read it again. "No, but it explains everything." She sank into a chair across from Brad, who was now snoring. Thank the goddess. "When we met, he had a lot of questions about my family. Namely Krista and her husband. I just thought he wanted to get to know me better."

"Then why does she have a stash like that here?"

Idiot or suicidal, he texted.

I glared admonishingly. Not that I disagreed. "My cousin's too vain to be suicidal. There has to be another reason."

"And I promise you, Brad has something to do with it," Mom said.

"His phone." I reached into his back pocket, took out his phone, and held it up to his unconscious leathery face. "Maybe they've been texting."

The phone opened, and I scrolled through the texts. Mom stood behind me to watch, as did the warlock, and I tried not to be overly pleased.

"Okay, no Krista, but he was texting someone with the initials KD."

"Krista Diaz," Mom said. "Click on it."

"Most of the texts have been deleted, but this is interesting."

Is it set? KD texted.

Everything's set. Where's the shipment?

It's hidden. You'll get it when I'm safe. But you better hurry. It won't take long for him to figure out I never crossed the border.

I sank into a chair. "Mom, was *she* a courier for the cartel?"

Mom collapsed into the seat beside me. "Her husband must've put her up to it. Think about it. A clean-cut business-woman in her forties. She'd never be suspected at the border checkpoint."

I nodded as my phone dinged.

She wanted out.

"Yes," I said, showing the text to Mom. "But she knew too much. She knew she'd be killed."

"And Brad promised to keep her safe," Mom said.

"For a price."

The warlock nodded, deep in thought himself.

"So she steals a million-dollar shipment of cash?" Mom asked. "She really is crazy."

"I'm not so sure. Why did she hide the money from him?"

"Maybe she figured out she couldn't trust him as far as she could throw him."

"That's my guess, too."

Red and blue lights flashed on the windowpanes as two cop cars pulled to the front of the house.

"They're here," I said to Mom, a little worried about her. This was not going to be easy for her, no matter how much she'd cooperated with the cops. There would be a lot of questions from a lot of people.

"How are we going to explain him?" she asked.

I hurried to a sidebar and took a bottle of whiskey down. After sprinkling some in his hair and shirt, I said, "He drank too much."

"And the money?" she asked.

Once again, I turned to the evilest person in the room, barring Brad.

He shrugged as though leaving it up to me.

Mom started to panic, not knowing what to do. "It's cartel money. Maybe we should call the DEA directly."

"And you have their number?" I asked her, teasing.

She pursed her lips at me. There was the mother I knew and loved. And was a little afraid of.

"Okay, you deal with them and I'll call the chief. He'll know what to do."

Before I could bring up his number, one of the cops knocked on the front door. Mom opened it, and two uniforms walked inside, which surprised me. Considering the charges, wouldn't they have sent a detective?

They ignored the unconscious man at the table and glanced around the place, taking Mom in first, then me.

The female officer nodded toward me. "You Krista Diaz?"

Shit. "I'm her cousin. She's out of town."

"Where out of town?"

I drew in a deep breath, trying not to wet myself, and said, "Mom, I don't think these are the cops."

Chapter Eight

I wish I was as thin as my patience.
—Fact

Mom and I sat at the table, hands tied behind our backs as the fake cops-slash-cartel lapdogs, four of them total, tore the place apart. Krista's husband must've figured it out sooner than she'd hoped.

One of the men hefted the duffle bag onto the table in front of us, the loud thud stirring Brad. I was going to kill him if they didn't. He went back to snoring while Mom sat in utter panic. I did, too, but that drama class was finally kicking in.

"It's not here," the guy said. "This is all I found. She must've stashed the rest."

A dread like I'd never felt began to creep into my bones like ice. "Are you real cops?" I asked the woman sitting with us at the table.

She smiled at me, and the breath fled my lungs like I'd been punched. They were really cops and they were on the cartel's payroll. There was no way we were walking out of here alive, unless it was to dig our own graves in the desert.

Sensing something amiss, Mom cast me a quick questioning glance.

I shook my head and closed my eyes to think. I was a charmling, damn it. I could shift into a bird, if nothing else, and go get help. In the meantime, they'd kill my mom and most likely Brad.

"What's his deal?" the officer asked, gesturing toward the man snoring away in front of her. She had curly red hair pulled into a bun and bright blue eyes.

"He's drunk."

"Obvs." She wrinkled her nose in distaste as my gaze traveled to the warlock sitting on the island, his back resting against a pillar on one side.

He was super busy examining his fingernails as though he hadn't a care in the world. We were about to die, and he was giving himself a manicure.

Surely he could do something. He'd pushed the man off me at the landfill. He may be incorporeal, but he could use his powers for good. The evil bastard.

I tried to get his attention with a mean facial expression, but he didn't bite. Then I cleared my throat. Really loudly. He didn't flinch. I couldn't take it any longer. I glared at him and said, "You really are evil, aren't you?"

The officer sat up on full alert and scanned the kitchen while the warlock—the one I'd had such high hopes for—grinned. Yet he couldn't be bothered to tear his gaze away from the task at hand.

"You could do something, you know."

Another of the officers walked into the dining room and asked his partner, "Who's she talking to?"

The woman got up to search the area.

"Who are you talking to?" the man asked when the woman didn't answer him.

I sank back into the chair with a loud sigh, giving up on him. "A warlock, if you must know. But don't worry. He's not the least bit concerned for my safety."

"Not the least?" Mom asked, deflating.

"Apparently not."

He grinned while examining yet another nail. For real?

"There's no one in here," the woman said from the kitchen. "I'll check the backyard."

The man nodded, then looked down at me. "Shut the fuck up if you don't want to die."

One corner of my mouth lifted at the threat.

"You think I'm funny?"

I looked up at him. He had rich umber eyes and pitted cheeks. "I doubt I'm going to live much longer either way."

He tilted his head to one side. "You're pretty calm about it."

"Not really," I said, the crack in my voice finally getting the warlock's attention.

"Okay, let me put it another way. Shut the fuck up or you won't die quick."

The warlock's jaw worked hard under the strain of his emotion, but he went back to his nails regardless.

"How's that for incentive?" he asked.

"Better."

The man waited impatiently for his partner to return when another officer walked in from the garage. "Bro, I'm telling you, it's not here. I don't know where she hid it, but there is a weird ass statue in one of the bedrooms. Maybe she stuffed it in there."

The first officer raked a hand through his short black hair.

When the subordinate asked, "Want me to break it?" I almost lost my shit. They were going to break my cousin into pieces. No matter how much I disliked her, I couldn't allow that to happen.

"Nah," the leader said, studying the back door. "It's not nearly big enough to hold all that cash."

I almost wept in relief.

The warlock peered out the window, grinned, then winked at me.

Hope blossomed. Did he have a plan after all? Did he call for backup? And if so, how?

I didn't have to wait long for an answer. To the first couple of questions anyway. Two men dressed in tactical gear stole out from my mother's bedroom and slid through the hallway like ghosts. They snuck up on the two officers in the dining room without making a sound, and I couldn't help but be impressed. Before the officers had a chance to react, two rifles had been trained point-blank at their heads.

The leader slid his hand onto his duty weapon anyway, as though in reflex, but the tactical officer pressed the tip of his rifle to the back of his head. "I wouldn't," he said, and I'd never loved two words more in my life.

In the next few minutes, SWAT spilled into the house. The team freed me and my mom while securing the corrupt officers and leading a drowsy and handcuffed Brad to a waiting van.

Knowing the officers' careers were over was almost enough to make me smile, but the adrenaline coursing through my veins was making me nauseous. I fought the bile in the back of my throat as my mom hugged me for a solid ten minutes, and I was so not a hugger. Her body shook uncontrollably.

I looked at the warlock. He was still doing his nails, and a smile finally broke free.

The captain of the SWAT team sat at the table with us. He had salt-and-pepper hair, skin the color of wet sand, and kind eyes. And he looked amazing in tactical gear. "You two okay?"

Mom nodded. "But you need to look in the closet of that room." She pointed from over my shoulder, refusing to release my neck.

"Yeah?" he asked, interested. "What's in there?"

"Move the shelves in the back of the closet," I said. "There are millions in cartel money."

His gaze snapped back to me. "It's in the closet?"

"It's a long story," Mom said. "I've been working with a Detective Hatch at Maryvale. He knows everything."

The man's face fell, and he lowered his head.

"What?" she asked.

He drew in a deep breath and refocused on her. "Detective Hatch was killed tonight in a car accident."

She covered her mouth with one hand.

"I'm sorry," he continued. "He was one of the good ones."

"It wasn't an accident, was it?"

"We suspect not," he said, pressing his lips together.

Her breath hitched in her chest, and I pulled her tighter.

Then the warlock's strange behavior resurfaced in my mind. I looked at the island, but he was gone, so I turned back to the captain. "How'd you end up here?"

"Now that's an interesting question." He turned to speak softly with one of his men, then turned back to us. "We got a phone call from a police chief in Salem, Massachusetts, of all places. Says he knows you?"

I laughed, wondering how he knew before it hit me. The warlock. Did he text the chief like he'd been texting me? If so, I'd love to know what he said to make him send in the cavalry.

"Yes," I said, shaking my head. Deph was probably beside herself. I'd need to hunt down my phone ASAP. The corrupt officers took them from us.

"Well, he was very persuasive."

A soft laugh escaped me. "He has that effect on people."

The man the captain had spoken to earlier stepped out of

Krista's room and nodded. "You might want to take a look for yourself, Cap."

A childlike grin stole across the captain's handsome face. "This I gotta see."

"Enjoy," I said.

Seconds later, we heard a loud whistle coming from Krista's room. He came out, his grin now more shit-eating than childlike, and sat back at the table. "Someone is going to miss that. Speaking of which, I got you two set up in a hotel for the next couple of nights. The cartel could come looking for their missing Jacksons."

"Well, there are a lot of them," I said in the cartel's defense.

"Any thoughts on where your niece is?" he asked mom.

She shook her head. "I have no idea, but I do know she had planned on turning that money over to the detective I'd been talking to." Even in her state of shock, she could lie with the skill of a seasoned actor.

"Okay, well, I'll have one of my men take you to the hotel." Before he could give the order, an officer rushed up and spoke softly to him. He didn't hesitate. He whistled to his men to gather and went out front to organize what looked like a search. "Call in the chopper, damn it," he said through clenched teeth.

When he walked back inside, I asked, "What's going on?"

He shook his head. "Brad Gaines slipped past the uniforms."

Mom gasped and eased closer to me. "He got away?"

"He did. I'm sorry, ma'am. Seems the EMT thought he was still out and left him alone in the ambulance for a few minutes. It was all the time he needed."

If that was the case, I wondered how long he'd been awake at the table. Had he heard our conversation? Did he know Mom had been working with a detective?

"We'll find him, but for now, I need you two off premises."

*　*　*

After Mom packed an overnight, I grabbed my luggage, then proceeded to answer frantic questions from Deph and the gang all the way to the hotel and then some more once we got checked in. Gigi seemed the most upset. "Is everyone there okay, Sarru?" she asked for the thousandth time, using the title I was still not comfortable with.

"We're fine," I assured her yet again.

"And... everyone is, you know, alive?"

"Are you worried that I killed someone?" I asked, slightly appalled.

"No! Not at all. Maybe a little."

I laughed. "I'll have you know, I drugged Brad without killing him, so take that, Debbie Downer."

She released an audible sigh. "I'm not worried about anyone but you, Sarru. I know if there was an accident, you'd never forgive yourself."

She had me there. "Thank you, Gigi."

"And the warlock?" she asked almost hesitantly. "He's still hanging around?"

"He is, though I haven't seen him since SWAT got here. But he saved our lives, Gigi. I'm certain he was the one who texted the chief."

"Actually, I think his intentions may have been even more noble."

"In what way?" I asked.

"I'm not certain just yet. I'll explain when you get back."

"However it happened, thank you so much, Chief."

"Thank the person who texted me. I wasn't sure if I should believe him at first, but he was rather insistent."

Funny, the captain said much the same thing. "Did he happen to give you a name?"

"In a way. Warlock. As in your warlock?"

"I'm assuming. He can't speak, but he can text lightning fast. It's crazy."

"Well, I'm just glad you're okay."

"Thanks. You guys get to bed. You're two hours ahead of us there. Or maybe three. I can never keep up."

"You, too," Deph said. "And try to stay out of trouble."

"You're one to talk."

We said our goodbyes, and I turned to see my mom already asleep.

A knock sounded at the door. It was the SWAT officer who'd driven us over. I hesitated, but it wasn't like he didn't know we were in there. I opened the door to the fresh-faced kid.

"The captain ordered you guys some food."

"Wow, thanks," I said, taking the bag from him.

"He also said to tell you not to blow anything up."

Oh, yeah. He'd definitely been talking to the chief. "Can you let him know that I haven't blown anything up in days?"

The officer's mouth formed an O, not sure what to say to that.

"No, wait, weeks," I said, amending my statement with an index finger in the air. "And he can take that to the bank."

His brows slid together. He was young and, as a Gen X, I didn't speak millennial. Or French. Sadly. So, I let it go.

He waved an uncertain goodbye. "Well, enjoy."

"Thanks." Even though I hadn't eaten in hours, I couldn't imagine taking a single bite. My stomach was too fragile at the moment.

I changed into a Dallas Stars jersey and plaid boxers for bed and crawled into the queen next to the window. The Phoenix lights comforted me, so I kept the curtains open to look at them. The familiar sound of Mom's soft snoring should have lulled me to sleep, but it didn't. Even after I'd just lived the longest day of my life, from catching a flight at five a.m. to catching an attempted murderer twelve hours—give or take—later. And yet, I lay there for two hours, unable to sleep. Dark hair, radiant blue eyes, wide shoulders, and a slim stomach kept me awake. Also the fact that I'd turned my cousin into a statue, but I was eighty-three percent certain I could rectify that situation. Maybe even eighty-four.

No, it was definitely the warlock. Those eyes. And the shoulders. And his hands. Holy mother of god, his hands. Masculine and elegant at once. I grabbed my phone and did something crazy. I texted him back. It was stupid. I knew it was stupid. This was the bad-boy fantasy I'd had in high school—and pretty much every year after that—all over again. Only this boy was truly bad. There were few things on earth more dangerous than a warlock. A T-rex, maybe, but those weren't much of a concern these days.

Also, he didn't have a phone. Not that I saw anyway. How could he receive a text? Yet, in my infinite wisdom, I did it anyway. I texted him. Like the nincompoop I was.

I typed slowly. Meticulously. Not sure what to say. In the end, I went for less is more. *You saved my life.*

I received his reply a split second after I hit send. It startled me so much I almost jumped off the bed. How the hell did he do that?

Actually, I didn't, he said.

I sat up and looked around. Nope. No warlock that I could see. So, I typed back. *What do you mean?*

I simply saved you from a lifetime of regret.

Had Gigi been right? Had his intentions been more noble than saving our lives? Because that was pretty damned noble in my book. *What do you mean?*

Tomorrow. Get some rest.

I'm trying. It's not working.

He sent a thinking face emoji.

How are you getting my texts?

Who says I am?

I stilled. Was he watching me text? Was he here? I looked around again but still couldn't see him. Maybe he could make himself invisible even to me.

The best way to find out was to ask. *Can you make yourself invisible to me?*

He didn't answer for a few torturous seconds, and when he did, he was very cryptic. *Does it matter?*

Filling my lungs to capacity to buy some time, I asked him aloud, "Are you here?"

Again, no answer for a solid minute, then, *I am.*

"Then show yourself."

He appeared instantly. Standing at the window, he watched the lights glisten along the horizon, his profile the most perfect I'd ever seen.

I had so many questions, I didn't know where to begin, so I charged ahead with some of the more basic ones. "Where are you? I mean, where is your corporeal body?"

My phone dinged. *Very far away.*

Vague much? "So, like, Alaska?" When he didn't answer, I guessed again. "Siberia?" Still nothing. "Hell?"

You're getting warmer.

My lungs stilled in my chest. He didn't look... I mean, I never thought... "Are you dead?" The implications of that hit me hard. No clue why. It wasn't like we could go on a double date with my bestie and her new fiancé. Warlocks were not widely accepted in the witch world.

He turned ever so slightly and smirked. *Only on the inside.*

The breath I'd been holding rushed out. "Good. I mean, you know, I thought I was losing what little grip I had on my powers already, because you don't look dead. I've noticed the departed have a certain monochrome finish to them. And they don't look solid, not entirely, but you"—I circled the air with an index finger, gesturing to pretty much all of him—"you're definitely solid."

The smirk turned wolfish, and a ferocious heat exploded inside me. My neck and cheeks grew hot. As did other parts.

I lunged for the light. "Well, okay, then. Good night." I pulled the covers up to my chin just as my phone dinged.

I can see perfectly in the dark.

Of course he could. "Oh," I said with an airy giggle. "What's to see? Just a girl trying to get some sleep after an exhausting day. Nothing interesting here."

I beg to differ.

When I looked back, he was no longer at the window, but sitting in a tub chair by a rather hideous floor lamp. I could just barely make out his outline. His perfect proportions. His mussed coiffure with every hair in its place.

Oddly enough, the more I watched him, the heavier my lids grew. "You can't sleep in that chair," I said softly. "It'll kill your neck."

He didn't answer. I held my phone to my chest with both hands, afraid I'd miss a text from him, but the last thing I remembered before falling into oblivion was a deep, silky voice saying, "You'll do just fine."

Chapter Nine

Next time I say, "Watch this,"
get me the fuck out of the bar.
—Meme

You'll do just fine. Did he really say that or had I been dreaming? If he could talk, why all the texts? Why all the mystery? His voice was amazing if it was him. Deep. Smooth. As silky as cool satin sheets on a warm night.

Mom's voice, which was neither deep nor particularly smooth, broke into my thoughts. "I just don't think this is a good idea."

"I can't come to town and not see him," I said to my mom. We were packing up after a very restful night, strangely enough. He was gone when I woke up, though. I was a little sad until I looked in the mirror. Sound sleep and corkscrew hair were like gasoline and fire. And if he did say that, what did he mean? I'd do just fine. With what? Was he really planning on enslaving me? Stealing my powers for another, lesser witch? One he could control?

"I understand that," Mom said. "Just go without me."

I put down my leave-in conditioner, waved a hand in the air to clear the cloud around my head, and faced her. "Mother, I am not leaving you alone. Not with my stepdad on the lam." The captain had called bright and early to check on us. They still hadn't caught Brad, which seriously put a damper on the cuz situation. We had to get back to the house and somehow load her into the truck my mom had secured. The obstacles were already insurmountable. Would the cops still be there? Would the house be taped off? Would we even be allowed back in? Add to that Brad and his penchant for asshattery, and I had no idea how we were going to get her loaded.

On the bright side, he had a uniform deliver my mom's crossover to the hotel and leave the keys at the front desk. I would say it was because Phoenix cops were the most considerate, but we did just make the man's career. It's not every day a SWAT team uncovers millions in cartel money.

"Please, stop calling him that, Annette. It's giving me a headache."

I tried not to grin. I failed. That'd teach her.

"Let's do that first. Besides, we have to go in and give our statements."

After scrunching my hair into a semi-manageable shape that didn't differ terribly from that of a tumbleweed, I sat beside her on the bed. "Mom, you and Dad have always gotten along so well. Why don't you want to stay with him? It's just for a little while."

She'd been filing a broken nail. She stopped and heaved a despondent sigh. "I don't want him seeing what a mess I've made of my life. Again."

"He can't possibly think that."

"Sure he can."

I patted her hand. "How do you know?"

"Because the last time I saw him, which was almost two years ago after Caleb stole ten thousand dollars out of my bank account and ran off with that mortician who dyed her hair to match the colors of the sun setting on the sea, he said, 'Made a mess of your life again, eh?'" She'd lowered her voice and changed her accent to match his, and I wanted to laugh. I didn't, but I wanted to.

"Oh, yeah. I forgot about Caleb."

She gaped at me. "After he stole ten thousand dollars from me?"

I winced. "Sorry. I thought that was Philip."

"No." She elbowed me softly. "Philip was the one who hocked your great-grandmother's diamond necklace to pay off his gambling debts."

"Oh, right." So many men, so few scruples. "Still, I really liked him."

"Me, too. Is he here?"

"Philip? I hope not. The only thing I have of value are these bracelets that I just kind of woke up with yesterday. Well, that and my right kidney. My left one hasn't been pulling her weight."

She grabbed my wrist and studied one of the silver vines wrapped around my wrists. The vines without a clasp to remove them, which I found out when I went to take a shower. "I was talking about your new best friend. You just woke up with these?"

"Yep." I held it up to the light and watched it sparkle. "I'm telling you, Mom, the things that happen in that house."

"Well," she said, putting her file away and standing up straight, chin held high like she was about to walk to her own execution, "let's get this over with."

"That's the spirit."

Thirty minutes later, we were standing on my dad's dilapidated front porch. Unlike Mom, Dad wasn't much for change. He tended to stay put. He'd lived in the same house since they divorced over thirty years ago.

We didn't warn him of our impending arrival. I wanted to surprise him. Also, I didn't know if he would want to see me. The last time we spoke, I told him he needed to get out more. Apparently, that was the wrong thing to say.

I knocked on the door, hoping he was home. He still worked, but only part time, and his maroon pickup was sitting in the driveway. When he didn't answer, I peeked in a cracked window. He was sitting in this living room, reading. I tapped on the glass.

Without looking up, he yelled, "You can come in. Your mother may not."

"See?" Mom said. "I told you this would not work."

She started to storm off. I stopped her by grabbing her arm and pulling her full circle until we both faced the door again. I opened it and said, "Dad, we need your help."

He looked over his half-moon glasses at me. "Would this have anything to do with the mess your mother got herself into yet again?"

"What mess?" Mom asked.

He pointed to the TV that was turned on, but the sound was off. "It's been all over the news."

"What?" She walked to a recliner, sank onto it, and watched as the screen flashed pictures of her house. "They said my name?"

"No, but tell me that's not your house. I dare you."

She deflated, but I was more interested in how he knew. "How did you know that's Mom's new house? She's only lived there a couple of months."

His mouth opened to answer, then he tore off his glasses and slammed it shut again.

I knew it!

"Dad, have you been scoping Mom out?"

Mom blinked in surprise.

"I happened to see her in the yard one day."

"Yes, because Mom is known for her stellar yard work."

"Annette," Mom said, slapping my arm. Or trying to. I dodged her hand with ease as Dad unfolded to his full six foot four and pulled me into a hug, knowing my sketchy history with hugs. But it felt wonderful. I sank against him, now understanding why I never got any of his height.

He stood me at arm's length. "How have you been, Annie Pot Pie?"

No way would I ever tell this man he was not my biological father. He was even better. He was everything a girl could've asked for. To say I was a daddy's girl growing up would've been a vast understatement. "I'm good. Sorry I haven't called in a while."

He nodded to Mom. "Dolores."

She raised her chin a visible notch. "Joe."

It was not lost on me that my parents had the same names as Dolores Claiborne and her husband Joe in one of my favorite Stephen Kings. Or the fact that my parents called me Annie. While I could be a little obsessive about fictional characters, I would never kidnap my favorite author and hobble them. That just seemed counterproductive in the long run.

"So, you gonna fill me in?" he asked Mom, gesturing for us to sit.

She crossed her arms over her chest and refused to talk, so I had no choice. Twenty minutes later, Dad sat in utter shock, shaking his head at Mom. And I'd left out most of the good stuff. He did not need to know about his niece's current state.

"I told you," Mom said, defending herself. "I figured out what he was up to. I was working with the cops."

"But he got away, Dad. We need her to stay here for a few days."

"You just happened to show up in the middle of this mess?"

For the first time, or maybe just the first time I paid attention, I felt him before I saw him. The warlock. He appeared seconds after I felt him, standing at the front window, looking out with his arms crossed over his chest, as usual. Dressed to the nines, also as usual, he wore the black button-down and slacks that molded to a set of slim hips and steely buttocks.

It was weird how much I was growing accustomed to his presence. How much I looked forward to it when he was gone. How much I craved those tiny glimpses at him I stole every chance I got.

I blinked back to Dad. "Yes, and I'm glad I did. I wouldn't have wanted Mom to go through that alone."

I also left out the fact that Team Deph and I had helped the police find Apple James, so when he asked "Mind telling me how you found a missing girl no one else could find?" I was more than a little stunned. "Security footage. It's all over the internet."

"I'm famous? Wait, does anyone else know it was me?"

"Not that I can tell. You always said you were psychic, but once a month you also claimed your ovaries were possessed by a rare tropical punch demon. It was difficult to take your claims seriously."

"That was just a phase, Dad. And I'm no more psychic than my ovaries are possessed."

"Then how did you find the girl?"

I filled my lungs and decided to throw my BFF under the bus. "Deph. She's a very powerful type of witch called a charmling, and she can find missing things. I gave her a call and voila. She found Apple in no time." I didn't lie so much as keep my part out of it.

The warlock tossed a knowing grin over his shoulder, while my dad just stared at me, probably trying to decide if I was messing with him or not. Apparently giving up, he slapped his hands on his knees and stood. "Okay, you get the couch," he said to Mom. "I don't have a bed in the spare room."

I stood, too. "Thanks, Dad."

Mom cleared her throat. "I appreciate it."

He nodded and gave her a rather interesting once-over, especially when he said, "You look good."

My heart leapt when she swallowed hard and said, "You do, too."

Did I sense the spark of young love? I turned before they saw the cartoon hearts bursting out of my eyes. Crazy kids. "Okay, we'll be back this afternoon. Will you be here?"

"I'll be here. How about we have dinner tonight?"

"I'd love that."

"Thank you, Joe," Mom said. "Nothing too—"

"Spicy. I remember." When a sly grin slid across his handsome face, I fought the urge to stuff my fist into my mouth and scream. I could feel the room get hotter. Could my parents actually have feelings for each other? Well, again.

Mom and I headed for the station to give our statements, and I couldn't have kept the grin off my face if I'd tried. My parents. In love. After all this time.

"What?" Mom asked at last. "Why do you keep smiling?"

I took a left and used the opportunity to turn away and try to ditch the creepy smirk. "Do I need a reason to smile?"

"Yes, ma'am, in my car you do."

She totally knew. I looked at our passenger in the rearview, his gaze locking with mine for a split second before I remembered to pay attention to the road. "I'm just happy to be alive, Mom. And you'd be surprised how often I've said that over the last few months."

"Me, too. This was all worth it to find that sweet little girl."

"Speaking of which, I'm going to run by the hospital first if that's okay."

"To check on her? Will they let you see her?"

"Maybe not, but I'd like to at least get her a gift."

"Of course."

Unfortunately, a uniformed officer stopped us before we could get to her room. "It's okay," I said, handing him the bright pink bag I got at the gift shop. "Can you make sure she gets this?"

"You can put it there." He pointed to a table stacked high with flowers and gifts for Apple.

"Thanks." I stopped to write a note on the card I bought.

Mom handed me a pen. "I was hoping you'd get to see her before you leave."

"Me, too. But that's okay. She's doing well. That's all that matters."

I wrote a note wishing her well and put the bag on top of a huge stuffed unicorn.

"What did you get her?"

Mom had gone to the bathroom while I shopped. "A tiny Betsey Johnson clutch with pink hearts all over it." Who knew I'd find Betsey in a hospital gift shop? The warlock raised a brow when he saw the price. He took it a notch higher when I picked up two.

"She'll love that," Mom said.

"Right?"

"Did you buy yourself one as well?" she asked, a knowing smirk on her face.

Heat rose up my neck at having been caught. "I may have."

"You never could resist that woman."

"I love her, Mom. You can't fight what's in your heart. Love is blind and all that shit." I folded my arm into Mom's and steered us toward the elevators when a woman's voice stopped me midstride. "Excuse me?"

We turned and the woman, a beautiful young mother holding a baby, stood in the hallway by the officer. She simply had to be Apple's mom. Same gorgeous skin. Same centuries-old eyes.

"You have to be Apple's mother."

The woman's eyes shimmered with unspent tears. Did she recognize me from the security footage Dad had talked about? It had to be from the landfill. I could only pray they didn't catch my magic act. No idea how I would explain the crow thing.

"Please call me Shari."

An older woman walked up behind her and had the same reaction to me.

"Let me guess. Grandma Lou?"

They both bent at the waist. "Sarru," the older woman said, and I almost gasped aloud.

"Sarru?" Mom asked.

I glanced at her. "It's a title of sorts." I turned back to them. "But not one I'm entirely comfortable with."

The smile that lit Shari's face was beyond priceless. "I would suggest, if I may, Sarru, that you get used to it."

A laugh escaped, despite my best efforts to contain it. "I'm beginning to get that. How did you know?"

"Word travels fast in our world."

"You practice the craft?"

"We do. We belong to a coven here in Phoenix."

From what I could tell, they couldn't see the warlock. Thank the goddess for small favors. "I want you to know it was actually my best friend, Defiance, who found Apple."

"We know. And we know what you did, too. You risked discovery to save our baby. We are more grateful than you can imagine. Our coven tried everything. The fact that you showed up when you did…" Her voice cracked, and her mother put an arm around her waist. "You were a gift."

"Thank you. I wasn't so sure there for a while. Deph had a difficult time finding her. Almost like she was blocked."

Shari nodded. "We never imagined something like this would happen when we cast the spell."

I led them to a row of chairs in the hall and gestured for them to sit. "The spell?"

The older woman took the baby while Shari explained. "We cast a spell years ago. Apple's father is… not a very nice person. Among other transgressions, he tried to take her out of the state once without informing me, so the judge revoked his right to see her. We were afraid he would try to kidnap her, so we cast a spell to keep her safe. To keep her biological father from finding her."

I tried to ignore the warlock standing over Apple's grandmother, gazing lovingly at the baby in her arms. "Ah. And that blocked Deph as well. And me. Deph said I should've been able to feel her, but I couldn't."

"You don't know how sorry we are," Grandma Lou said.

"Don't be," my mother said, taking all of this in stride. "You had no idea something like this would happen."

I couldn't help a peek at the baby wrapped in yellow and blue. "A boy?"

Shari nodded. "Sarru, we would be so honored if you could bless him."

I leaned back in surprise. "Bless him?"

"And Apple." She lowered her head. "I know it's asking a lot."

"Of course it's not. I've just never done anything like that."

"I can tell you how, Sarru," Grandma Lou said, her expression full of hope, "if I may be so bold."

The warlock watched me, waiting for my answer as well.

After a very long moment of hesitation, I finally said, "I would be honored. Is she awake?"

"She is. She's asking for more ice cream. She's already had three containers."

I laughed. "Good for her."

Mom and I followed the women past the uniform and into Apple's room, but I didn't dare come empty-handed. I had a half pint of ice cream in each hand. I didn't know what to expect. Would she remember seeing me? Talking to me?

When I walked up, she certainly didn't seem to, so I didn't mention it.

Her mother gestured me closer. "Apple, this is the woman who helped find you."

The sweet girl looked tiny in the hospital bed. She still wore a neck brace due to swelling in her spine from the hit-and-run, and the side of her face had been scraped raw, just like her incorporeal image had been. I was still processing it all, everything she'd been through, when Apple held out her hand.

"Oh, right." I rushed forward, took the lid off one of the ice creams, and handed it to her.

Her mouth widened across her beautiful face as she took the spoon from me.

"I'm so happy you're okay, Apple."

"Thank you," her mother said, prompting Apple to do the same.

"Thank you," she said, her voice little more than a barely audible croak. She said something else, but I couldn't hear her, so I leaned closer. "Can you really turn into a bird?"

"Oh," I said, leaning back, not sure how much her mother would want her to know. But she'd been through enough. She deserved the truth. "Yes. Yes, I can, Apple."

Her huge eyes rounded. "Can I see?"

I cast a worried frown at her mom. "Did your mom tell

you?"

"No." She laughed softly. "I told Mommy and Grandma Lou. I saw you, remember?"

After an affirming nod from Shari, I sat on the side of her bed. "You remember that?"

She nodded and took another bite.

"Then you've already seen me do it."

Disappointment furrowed her tiny brows. It was so cute. "I guess. But Mommy and Grandma Lou haven't."

She had a point. "How about you give me a call when you're out of the hospital, and we can arrange for a... special viewing." It would be my luck, however, for my powers to fizzle out with performance anxiety.

She brightened. "Deal."

"Are you ready?" Grandma Lou asked.

I nodded and proceeded to bless the kids under Lou's expert tutelage and the unwavering gaze of a warlock. But it didn't take long for a spell to find its way to the forefront of my mind. I drew it on the air over the baby and, just like before, a bright green light spilled from the lines of the spell. I repeated the spell over Apple. She watched the lights flare to life and the spell sink into her. She rubbed her tummy and giggled as though it tickled. I wouldn't be surprised.

"Thank you, Sarru," Shari said, bowing again as we left.

Mom studied me like a scientist would a lab rat.

"What?" I asked.

"They treat you like royalty."

"I guess. They do that to Deph and me both, now. It's so weird, Mom. I don't think I'll ever get used to it."

My mom stared at me for several minutes as we walked. She was so absorbed she nearly took out a nurse and a medicine cart at the same time. "It's like I don't even know you," she said when we got to the elevators.

I nodded. "Samesies, Mom. Samesies."

Chapter Ten

I feel a spree coming on.
Whether it's killing or shopping is totally up to you.
—Meme

Mom and I ran by the station to give our statements, and I prayed our stories would match. It was hard to figure out what to put in and what to leave out. I figured the part where I turned Krista into a statue was a definite omit, but the authorities hadn't made the connection between me and the landfill yet, so I didn't mention that either. As long as I left town in the very near future, I should be okay. The questions surrounding Apple and my part in her rescue were questions I did not want to answer at the moment.

Unfortunately, Brad Gaines was still at large, and very few of our questions had answers as of yet.

"But he targeted Krista," I said to the detective now in charge of the case, an older man with a killer comb-over. "He used my mother to get to Krista. How did he know about

Krista's situation with her husband? That she would want out?"

"We're still working on that, but he's been a con man his entire life. His rap sheet reads like pulp fiction. People like him are in it for the long game. He'd probably been planning the con for months and saw your mother as an easy in."

Mom lowered her head as though embarrassed.

"Mom, you saw through him, remember? You went to the authorities. You caught him."

"Too late to do any good, though."

"Are you kidding? He could have killed Krista when she turned over that money."

"Speaking of your cousin," the detective said, "you haven't heard from her, have you?"

I winced. "Not yet."

"If you do, please let me know. She's in serious danger. I'm worried either Gaines or her husband got to her."

"I don't know," I said, trying to put the detective's mind at ease, "she's pretty resourceful. And insanely hard-headed these days."

My mother pinched my thigh.

"I'm just saying," I just said, "once she puts her mind to something, she sticks to it. I bet she's sipping margaritas on a beach somewhere. Just trying to clear her hard—really hard —head."

Mom went in for another pinch, but I dodged her by jumping out of my chair. "If that's all, Detective?"

"For now. Again, let me know if you hear from her."

"Absolutely."

Mom went in for another pinch, but I hurried out before she could manage it.

After giving our statements, we ran by Twisters for a bite and then drove to the house to meet Mom's friend with the truck. I wondered if I should get a tarp to cover Krista with for the trip until I made a right off Elm and saw a vehicle sitting in the driveway.

I screeched to a halt in the middle of the street and stared.

"It's perfect," Mom said, patting my arm with the excitement of a chihuahua with an overactive thyroid. When I turned to look at her, my jaw gaping unattractively, she shrugged. "What? It's absolutely perfect."

It was around that moment I noticed the warlock laughing in the back seat. He covered his eyes with one hand, his shoulders shaking.

I refastened my jaw and glared at the woman who gave birth to me. "You cannot be serious."

"Annie, are you not seeing the beauty of this?"

"Beauty? I can't drive that thing across the country."

"It's actually quite comfortable."

I thought the warlock had disappeared again until I glanced over my shoulder and saw him laying across the back-seat, laughing uncontrollably. This was getting ridiculous. "Mother—"

"Don't mother me. You made this mess, young lady. You have to clean it up, and that begins with you getting your poor petrified cousin to Salem."

"My poor petrified cousin?" I screamed, reaching an octave only a dog could hear. And people wonder why I never married. "She was going to kill me!" A car behind me forced me forward. I had no choice but to pull into the driveway beside... it. "I can't believe this is happening."

Mom elbowed me. "He's getting out. Don't be rude."

I rolled my eyes. After she stepped out, I turned to the peanut gallery. "It's not that funny."

He shook his head in agreement, then doubled over again.

I ground my teeth together and decided to ignore him. It wasn't nearly as funny as he was making it out to be. It was, in fact, mortifying. Not that I didn't respect the profession, but never in my wildest dreams had I ever imagined myself driving a hearse. And a very dated one at that. The long black car with chrome moldings had to be at least fifty years old.

"You must be Annette," the man said through Mom's still-open door. A pudgy guy with thick glasses and killer sideburns, he looked like he'd just stepped out of a Quentin Tarantino film.

"That's me." I got out of the car at last and noticed a couple of Mom's neighbors spying on us. I could hardly blame them. After last night's fiasco with cops and SWAT swarming the place to a hearse in the driveway today, their curiosity was more than warranted.

He took my hand. "I'm Brain."

"Brian?"

He chuckled. "Nope, Brain. Like the character?"

"*Pinky and the Brain*?"

A salty frown hijacked his pleasant face. "*Escape from New York*."

"Oh, right. That's an oldie, huh?" When I got another frown for my efforts—no more small talk for me—I added, "But so good. One of my favorites."

"She'll get you there no problem," he said, indicating the hearse he was obviously quite proud of. "But how are you getting her back?"

I'd wondered that myself. "I'll have to ship it."

His head whipped around to me.

"Her. I'll have to ship her."

"You're just going to throw her on a truck like a piece of garbage?"

I tossed my hands into the air and glared at my mother. "That's it. I am not driving this thing all the way to Salem, especially with the Brain over there nitpicking every little detail." I headed for the front door when my mom stopped me.

"Annette Cheri Osmund, just how else do you plan on getting my niece there?"

"Your niece is dead?" Brain asked, the color draining from his already pasty skin. "You have to be licensed to transport a dead body."

"What? No," Mom said, laughing. "We had a statue of her made. Remember? And Annie needs to get her—it—to Salem pronto. It's kind of an emergency."

"You had a statue made of your niece?" The horrified look on his face cracked me up. On the inside. My outer parts were still fuming.

I looked over and saw the warlock leaning against the hearse, arms crossed over his wide chest. He did that a lot. Leaned. Crossed. Maybe he didn't have a lot of energy to spare while astral projecting so he had to use any available surface to rest against. Which made no sense whatsoever since he was incorporeal, but it was the only explanation I could come up with. Either that or he knew how fine he looked doing it. The position accentuated the expanse of his shoulders. The bulk of his biceps. The sinews of his forearms since he'd rolled up his sleeves.

As Mom tried to smooth things over with the Brain, I walked over to my new bestie.

Would he stay here now that his mission for me was over? Even if he did come back to Salem, he could never get inside Percy. That house was like the Fort Knox of the paranormal realm. Which was probably a good thing, what with him being a warlock and all.

"This is the worst day of my life," I whispered to him, being careful to leave at least five feet between us. No idea why.

He didn't answer. Probably because my melodramatic tendencies were not for everyone. But he did give me his full attention by watching me from underneath insanely thick lashes. I wondered how different he would look in real life.

Would the five o'clock shadow that framed his amazingly sculpted mouth be darker? More prominent? It couldn't possibly be any sexier.

"If all goes well," I said, changing the subject, "I'm leaving tonight."

He tilted his head ever so slightly, never taking his gaze off me. It gave me butterflies. I was way too old for butterflies.

"So, I guess it'll be goodbye soon."

Nothing. Just his rapt attention, which seemed to be focused primarily on my mouth at the moment.

"Can I ask what your name is? Or is that one of those things where, if I know your name, I have some kind of power over you?" I'd like some power over him. Lots of power over him. And a set of handcuffs. I waited for my phone to ding, but nothing. I lifted it to check just in case. Nada. "So, that's a no?"

He pulled half his lower lip between his teeth, making the dimples at the corners of his mouth appear, and the bones in my legs dissolved. In an attempt to retain what little composure I had left, I looked past him into the hearse and saw something inside. I leaned in closer, coming dangerously close to him. My mouth fell open when I realized what was inside. I stared, panting for a solid minute, then turned to Brain and pointed at the window. "Is that a freaking body?"

Brain chuckled and walked over.

Mom followed, trying to peek over his shoulder.

"It's a mannequin," he said. "You know, to give people a thrill when they look inside, which they always do." He turned to Mom. "Human nature and all."

I had a very hard time believing that, but Mom laughed and nodded in agreement. Freaking loons. I glared at her when Brain walked to the back to open it up. "Where did you find this guy?"

"Oh, we've been friends since high school."

"How come I've never met him?"

"Are you sure you haven't?"

I deadpanned her. "I think I would remember him."

Brain chuckled to himself. "Guess I should've taken Martha out at the house, eh?"

I groaned aloud.

Twenty minutes later, after borrowing a dolly from a neighbor, the three of us were struggling to get Krista in the back of the hearse. Brain had some kind of gurney that was supposed to be used to move bodies, but he said it had a flat tire. In other words, it was missing a wheel. Naturally. "But we can use it to get her into the coach," he said, cheerful as ever.

"Great."

In his defense, he'd been right. We were able to load Krista onto the gurney—with lots of huffing and puffing—and raise her up using a very cool lever until she was level enough with the floor to slide her inside.

I'd draped myself over the back of the driver's seat to pull her toward me, as the rollers in the floor were very old and uncooperative. The warlock sat in the passenger's seat and watched me. Or watched my ass, since it was impossible to miss.

"Oh, gosh," I whispered to Krista. "I hope we don't accidentally break off your head. Then again, it's not like you were using it. Seriously? You married a member of the cartel? Have you ever had even an ounce of common sense?"

Then again, I was thirsting after a warlock. I pinched the bridge of my nose. It must run in the family. My mom. Krista. Me. We were all suckers for the tall, dark, and most likely to commit a crime in broad daylight. You'd think, given our age and the status of our ankles, we'd grow out of it.

"You know, you could help," I said to the warlock as I pulled on the gurney.

He didn't answer. But when I got my hair caught in one of

the rollers, he did peek over the seat in mild interest. So, there was that.

"Can I ask you a question?" Brain asked.

I tugged at the lock of hair and winced when I heard strands rip. "Sure."

"Why did you buy a statue if you didn't have a way to get it back?"

"She's an impulse shopper," Mom said. She walked over, reached inside, and patted my back as though consoling me. "She's in therapy and taking medication. We have high hopes this time."

He showed a fist in solidarity. "Good for you. Stick with the program."

I nodded, my internal reaction somewhere between a laugh of wild abandon and an all-out ugly cry. Even if I did manage to get Krista back to Salem, I had no idea how to turn her back. "Thank you. I'll take good care of her."

"Patty," he said.

"Patty?"

"That's her name. Patty Hearse."

I fought the urge to rant about the inappropriate nature of that name but decided against it, knowing that whatever I said would go in one ear and out the other.

We finally got Krista secured, and the three of us—four counting the warlock—stood back and admired our work.

"I think we did good," Brain said.

Mom beamed at him. "I agree."

I wanted to cry. "If not for all the broken limbs and duct tape, I would totally agree."

Brain scrunched his nose at Krista's new disfigurements, and I had to wonder how those would translate into her human self if we did manage to turn her back.

"I don't know," Brain said. "We only broke off an arm, two toes, and a finger."

"Oh, no, I broke the finger earlier."

"See? Not too bad in my book."

As Mom and Brain discussed the particulars of how we would get the car back to him, I scooched closer to the warlock. "Okay, you're clearly more experienced at these things. Is she still in there? My cousin?"

He offered me the barest hint of a nod, and I didn't know if I should feel elated or sad.

"Can she... does she know what's going on? What's happened to her?"

One of his wide shoulders rose and fell in a half-hearted shrug.

"You don't know or you don't care?"

He grinned.

Mom waved as a friend of Brain's picked him up. "Thank you, again, Brain. And tell your mother she still owes me that camel."

I did not want to know. "I guess we should get to Dad's."

"I don't know, Annie." She looked at her house forlornly. "I think I'm okay to stay here."

"Do you? Let me ask the warlock."

She went completely still. "He's here?"

"He's here. What do you think, Mr. Warlock?"

He frowned at his new title.

"Ah," I said, absorbed in what he was telling me. Absolutely nothing, but Mom didn't need to know that. "He says, yes, you should absolutely stay here tonight. Alone. Unprotected. With a killer who happens to have a vendetta against you on the loose." I turned to her and added, "Not to mention a warlock skulking in the shadows."

"Your dad's it is." She ran to her crossover and jumped into the driver's seat as I tried not to giggle.

My phone dinged. I pulled up my messages and saw the familiar skulls and crossbones. "You're talking to me again?"

No reaction, so I read the text. *I do not skulk.*

I turned with as much sass as I could muster and whistled from over a shoulder as I walked to Patty's driver's side. "Looks like I struck a nerve."

He was already in the passenger's seat when I got inside, much to my delight, and he was pouting. Arms crossed over his chest, which was his usual MO, but he was looking straight ahead with his eyebrows furrowed so adorably I wanted to kiss him.

Him.

A warlock.

Who possibly wanted to enslave me for all eternity.

Deph was right. I needed to put my hormones aside and consider the situation with a level head. Then he turned to look at me as though wondering what was taking me so long.

"Sorry," I said, starting up the engine. Of a hearse. A hearse I was about to drive across the country. Gawd, I missed my Charger.

Chapter Eleven

I overheard someone order a margarita
after being told Diet Coke wasn't available,
which is similar to how I make most of my life decisions.
—Meme

All things considered, driving the hearse was fun in a creepy, Stephen King kind of way. I parked Patty down the street so Dad wouldn't see what I was driving and ask a lot of questions I didn't want to answer. Then I used Dad's shower to freshen up so I wouldn't have to get a hotel room until tomorrow night. I'd have to pull over for a power nap at some point, but no reason to get a hotel room just yet.

Dad grilled steaks and made baked potatoes. He was a simple guy. After a wonderful dinner, we talked for a couple of hours about everything from the lunar landing to K-pop, and I couldn't remember having a better time with my parents. Not since... since before Austin's disappearance.

I disentangled myself more and more from the conversation, giving them a chance to talk. To laugh. To get to know each other again. But they still seemed reserved around each other. There was a lot of pain there. A lot of resentment to get over. But if they loved each other, really loved each other, surely they could work it all out.

I excused myself and called Deph from the kitchen.

"You haven't texted all day," she complained with nary an *hola* for my efforts.

"No time for that. Quick, I need a love spell."

"What? No. Those never work. They always—*always*—backfire. Haven't you been studying?"

"Bro, what do you think I studied first? Just ask Gigi which herbs I need to spike my parents' food with to, you know, help them along."

"Your parents?" she asked in surprise.

"My parents."

"Nette, you can't force them to love each other again."

"Trust me. I won't be forcing anything. They're flirting, Deph. Like really flirting."

"No way."

"Way. Any thoughts?"

"Two, actually: tequila and lime."

"Oh, right," I said, realization dawning. "I didn't even think of that. They just need to loosen up a little and let nature take its course."

"Bull's-eye. So, have you seen the warlock again?"

I glanced over at the warlock standing in the doorway. "Nope. Not at all."

Though he pretended to be busy listening to my mother clammer on about the price of lettuce these days, one corner of his mouth rose as though he heard me.

"Are you sure?" Deph asked. "Because that's the same tone you use every time you try to cheat at gin rummy."

I gasped, pretending to be appalled. "I have never cheated

at gin rummy." When my outburst was met with absolute silence, I added, "I cheat at crazy eights. Never at gin rummy."

"Whatev, are you fibbing or not?"

I released a long, exhausted sigh. "Can I get back to you on that?"

"Annette," Deph said, clearly alarmed, "is he still hanging around?"

"Kind of, but I'm working on it."

"Dude, is he really hot enough to risk your life for?"

"It's not just about that, Deph. I mean, he is, but he helped me find Apple. He saved me from being caught naked in the middle of a landfill. And, *and*," I said, pausing for dramatic effect, "he likes babies."

"Of course he does!" she shouted far louder than necessary. "He's a warlock! What do you think they do with babies?"

Oh, hell no. I did not want that in my head. "Defiance," I said, my turn to be taken aback, "Gigi said it herself. There are some warlocks who are not all evil." When the warlock frowned, I added, "And I'm pretty sure he can hear every word we're saying."

I could sense the grinding of her teeth. Or maybe that was mine. "We can discuss this when you get home. When are you headed back?"

"I'm heading out tonight."

"This late?" she asked.

"I'll drive until I get tired and grab a hotel room for the night. I have forty hours of blacktop ahead of me."

"Wait, you're driving?"

Oops. "Didn't I mention that?"

"Annette," Deph said, her voice edged with warning, "why are you driving? No, wait, *what* are you driving?"

I thought of Patty. "You so do not want to know."

"Oh, I do. Trust me, hon. I want to know with every bone in my body."

"Can I just explain everything when I get back?"

It took her a while to answer. "Pinky swear? You'll tell me everything?"

"Pinky swear."

"And the warlock?"

"Okay, fine, I'll pinky swear with him, too, but I'm pretty sure he already knows everything."

"You're funny."

"I like to think so."

We hung up, and I went straight for the liquor cabinet. Also called the farthest kitchen cabinet on the left. Either way.

"What are you looking for?" Dad asked, walking up beside me.

"Tequila."

He made a sour face. "The last time I had tequila, I asked your mom to marry me."

"Then that is exactly what I need."

"Then I vomited for three days."

"Oh." I moved a bottle of God-only-knew-what aside and found the perfect substitution. "How about cinnamon schnapps?"

He lifted a shoulder. "Your mom loves that stuff."

"Then cinnamon schnapps it is." I grabbed the bottle and ferreted out a couple of shot glasses he got from Vegas.

"We're drinking it straight?"

"It's cinnamon. It'll be intoxicating and give you fresh breath. Win-win, baby."

He chuckled. "Are you trying to get me drunk?"

"What?" I went back to the dining room and set a glass in front of Mom. "Drink up, buttercup."

"Good heavens, Annie." She picked up the bottle and read the label. "Where did you find this?"

"In the liquor cabinet."

"I keep trying to tell you," Dad said, "I do not have a liquor cabinet."

I poured them each a finger's worth. "Is it a cabinet?"

"Yes," he said, coughing slightly, then sucking in a long breath to cool his throat.

"Is there liquor in it?"

"Yes," he said, gesturing for more.

"Well, there ya go."

Mom sniffed and let out a whistle before asking, "Aren't you having any?"

"Unlike you two," I said, grabbing my bag, "I have to drive."

"Wait, you're leaving now?"

"I am. Thanks for everything, Mom. I'll let you know if I find out more."

She stood. "Drive careful, Annie. I mean it. And text me every couple of hours."

"Will do. I'm going to check in with the captain's office every day. Hopefully they'll catch Brad soon." But not too soon. If my parents could really rekindle that spark they once had, they'd need all the time alone together they could get.

I let Mom hug me, trying not to scrunch up my nose, before heading toward the door.

Dad took my overnight and walked me to the hearse. The hearse! I forgot about the hearse.

"Why are you driving Patty?"

Dad knew Patty? Small world. "I bought a statue and borrowed her to get the statue home."

He peeked inside, but by that point, it was too dark to see anything. "A statue, huh?" It was almost like he didn't believe me.

"I'm in therapy. And taking medication."

"Right," he said, again, doubt suffusing every syllable. Admittedly, there was only the one.

"Is everything okay?"

He pressed his mouth together, his face mere shadows under the streetlamp. "I feel like something has changed and, to be frank, Annie, I'm worried you're not my little girl anymore."

Boy, did he hit the nail on the head, except for the little girl thing. I'd always be his little girl. At least in my mind. "Everyone changes, Dad. But our relationship won't."

He nodded to appease me. "I want you to know something."

"Okay," I said, growing wary.

It took him a moment to continue, and when he did, he had to look away. "Your mom and I were never perfect parents, but we've always loved you no matter what."

This conversation was growing exceedingly uncomfortable. And alarmingly similar to the one I'd recently had with Mom. "I know, Dad. I'm very grateful."

"No, I don't think you understand. You've always been special." He scoffed at himself. "I know every parent says that, but you really are. And it took me a long time to figure out why."

"Thanks?" I said, not sure if that was a compliment or not.

"I don't know what's going on in Salem, but I think it's big. Bigger than me or your mother. But I need you to understand something. Before any more time slips by, I need you to understand something important."

"Okay." My stomach clenched painfully. Perhaps it was the pessimist in me, but this did not sound good.

He drew in a deep breath and released it slowly, then said softly, "I've always known I wasn't your biological father."

I stared at him, absorbing what he just said before losing my shit completely. "Dad! How did you know? I just found out yesterday." When he narrowed his eyes at me, I said, "Well, okay, due to some rather... unusual occurrences, I've suspected for a couple of weeks now, but I didn't know for sure for sure until yesterday."

He pressed his lips together and nodded in thought.

"How long have you known?"

"Since the day your mother told me she was pregnant."

"Wow." I leaned against Patty. "That's a really long time."

"Hon, I'm telling you this now because no matter what happens, I want you to know that I don't care. I never cared. I have loved you from the moment you were born, despite all the gray slimy stuff you were covered in."

"That's so... sweet."

"I mean, it was hard to get past at first, but once they got you all cleaned up, you were like this little angry raisin and, well, I just fell in love."

"An angry raisin. That sounds like me."

"You do what you need to do. I'll take care of your mother. I have a feeling you have bigger fish to fry."

"Someday, you're going to have to explain to me how you know all of this."

The patient smile that spread across his face was familiar and yet, somehow, brand new. "Drive careful. And don't pick up any hitchhikers."

He'd been giving me that same set of instructions since I got my learner's permit. "Pinky swear. Unless he's hot."

He laughed softly and pulled me into a hug. I didn't mind at all.

After he walked back into the house, I turned a full circle, hoping for a little company on the road. The warlock was gone. I could've texted him, but it wasn't like I could invite him home with me. We'd have to part ways at some point no matter what. Maybe he hated goodbyes as much as I did.

"Looks like it's just me and you, Patty." I climbed behind

the wheel and set out for a little town called Salem, only freaking out a little when I saw Krista's statue in the rearview. But I kept doing it. About once every half hour, I would catch a glimpse of her unexpectedly and almost jump out of my skin. I kept wondering if she was conscious. Aware of what happened to her and watching me out of her calcified eyes. Plotting her revenge. Reveling in the thought of my demise.

After six hours of that shit, I'd had enough. I considered getting a hotel regardless of how spring fresh I smelled—Dad had great soap—but I decided against it for two reasons. One, I was flat-ass broke, and I didn't want to use the company credit card any more than I had to. And two, I didn't want to pull up to a hotel in a hearse. The looks on the road were enough. I horrified children. Unsettled adults. Confused cows. Or that was my take on the cows I saw trailered in Gallup. All in all, it was fantastic. I never knew the power I could wield over a person's sanity. I totally needed one of these babies for everyday use.

After barely putting a dent in my trip, I pulled into a casino parking lot outside of Albuquerque for a snooze. I stretched the zombie sunshade—Brain had quite the sense of humor—across the inside of the windshield, grabbed my parka to use as a pillow, and settled in for a quick nap. Just in case, however, I decided to set my alarm for two hours. That would put me back on the road before five, and I could get through Albuquerque before rush hour hit hard.

Instead of going to sleep, however, I lay there and thought of the one person I'd been trying not to think about the entire trip.

"I don't want to hear it," I said to Krista, in case she was trying to tell me what a loser I was. "I already know I'm a loser. I'm not pining over him. I'm just upset that he didn't say goodbye."

She didn't answer, which was fine. Actually, more than

fine. If she had answered, I would've flown out of that hearse so fast, I would've left vapor trails.

"Also, I'm sorry about the duct tape. It's all we had. I'll try to find something that matches a little better when we get home."

Thankfully, the car was so old that it had a single front seat for me to recline on. I stared out the driver's-side window at the flashing Route 66 Casino sign, refusing to think about him. Thus, thinking about him constantly, just like I did the entire trip. On the bright side, I figured I was safe for the time being. On the not-so-bright side, I would probably never see him again.

I cradled my phone and turned onto my side to block out the light. What felt like five minutes later, I checked my phone and shot upright. Nine a.m. How was it nine a.m.? I brought up my alarms. The one I'd set was turned off. I did that so often. Turned off my alarm without ever waking up. Damn it.

With nature calling me, her ringer turned up to eleven, I hit up a nearby convenience store to answer her call, wash my face, and brush my teeth. Then I grabbed an extra-large coffee and a breakfast sandwich and hit the road again. Thankfully, Brain had a really decent set of CDs. I hadn't used CDs in so long, I forgot how to work the player, but it all came rushing back fairly quickly. Not unlike the occasional memories of that acid trip I took once. At least Brain didn't install a cassette player. I didn't have a pencil eraser should tragedy strike.

For the next few hours, I chatted with Krista, making bets with her on how many out-of-state license plates we would see. Strange thing was, she won every time. We listened to a variety of music, ranging from Celtic and bluegrass to grunge and heavy metal, and debated the merits of each. Finally, around midnight, I decided to get a hotel. The shower and cool sheets were heavenly, and I only got a few strange looks about Patty.

But all the while, I debated texting the warlock. Over and

over, my hand went to my phone to see if he'd texted me, only to be disappointed yet again. And so went the next two days until I pulled into Salem very late one night. I called someone I hoped was an ally, hoping he would still be awake.

"Hey, Roane," I said to Deph's boy toy, infusing my voice with a lightness I did not feel. "I'm almost at the house. Can you meet me out front?"

"Sure thing."

"Oh, and bring a dolly?"

"A dolly?"

"Yes. Also, can we maybe keep this to ourselves for a while?"

"The part about the dolly?"

"No, all of it. I'll let Deph know I'm back tomorrow morning, but I have a couple of things to move into the house first."

"Such as?"

I took a right and headed down Chestnut to Percy. My beloved Percy. "My suitcase, for one."

"It was supposed to be a two-day trip. What the hell did you take?"

"I can get the suitcase, actually. I just need help with a statue I bought at a flea market."

"You bought a statue at a flea market?"

"See, it's a funny story." I pulled into the drive. Even in the dark, Percy was magnificent. A moss-green, ivy-covered manor with six gables forming a circle over the main part of the house and accented with a black roof and trim. I'd missed him. Maybe it had only been my imagination, but it seemed like he was warming up to me lately. The fact that Percy, aka Percival Channing Goode, was actually Defiance's grandfather was of little consequence. At least in my humble opinion. I stole a picture of him from when he and Gigi were dating back in the day. Curly black hair. Wide shoulders. Thick biceps. The pic was a sad testament to the fashion styles of the seventies, but that man had been hot before Gigi and her coven burned him in hellfire—at his behest—leaving her a widow and Percival the guardian of the house.

"And?" Roane asked, apparently still waiting for the funny story.

"I know you heard me pull up." Dude was a werewolf. He could hear a mouse hiccup from a mile away. "Can you just meet me out front already?"

"You've gotten bossier. I like it."

I tried not to blush. Talk about hot guys. Deph did well. Roane was gorgeous and kind and super protective. An alpha through and through. Also, he wore a leather kilt and hiking boots.

Trying not to study the guy engaged to my bestie like I was going for my PhD, I stepped out of the hearse, gave her a grateful pat on the roof, and waited for my backup.

A woman's voice crashed into my thoughts, and I froze when she said, "Care to explain exactly what the hell is going on?"

Chapter Twelve

*I just want my room clean enough so that if someone stops by,
it doesn't look like I'm six days into battling a poltergeist.*
—Sign on Annette's door

I spun around at the sound of my bestie's voice, the anger in it
as sharp as broken glass.

"And why the bloody hell are you driving a hearse?" She
stood on the front porch, arms crossed over her robe-clad
chest, an annoyed glower on her pretty face. A glower so
strong I could make it out despite the minimal light
emanating from a streetlamp.

"What are you doing out here?" I asked, my voice ear-
piercingly high. "Did that wolf rat me out?"

The porch light came on, flooding the area so I could see
Deph's glower much more clearly. Thank goodness.

"Every two hours," she said from between gritted teeth,
her blue eyes shooting razor-sharp daggers.

I smoothed my hair back and raised my chin a notch. "What are you talking about?"

"You promised to text me every two hours."

"I did!"

"The first day, yes. I haven't heard shit from you in two days. You haven't even responded to my texts. Or calls. Or the National Guard I sent out this morning." She looked up in thought. "I should probably call them back now."

None of that was true. I may not have texted every two hours, but I did respond to her texts. At least I thought I did. I had a lot on my mind. Namely a certain warlock who'd apparently abandoned me for greener pastures.

Before I could defend myself, Deph ran barefoot down the steps and slammed into me, the tackle hug not nearly as annoying as I expected it to be. I even laughed and hugged her back. "I'm sorry. I didn't think you meant for me to take the every-two-hour thing literally."

"First," a male voice said from behind Deph, "I did not rat you out. Though I may have had you on speakerphone."

"Of course you did," I said into Deph's hair.

"And second, if you two are finished, where's this statue?"

Deph finally released me, setting me at arm's length. "You saved lives, Annette. Lives!"

Her pride-filled gaze was almost more than I could bear. I couldn't tell her about Krista. Not just yet. I couldn't disappoint her so soon after making her so proud. "Excuse me, but *we* saved lives. I couldn't have done any of that without you and Gigi and the chief."

"Whatev." She peeked over my shoulder, trying to see inside Patty's darkened interior. "You bought a statue? For real?"

"Yeah, well, you know. When you see a piece you love, it's all downhill from there."

She deadpanned me as Roane went around and opened Patty's rear end. "You're a collector now?"

"Right?" I said, offering an airy laugh. "It just hit me out of the blue. Art imitates life, after all. Who knew?"

When her eyes narrowed and she started toward Patty's read end, I tried to head her off. I failed, damn her long legs. "You know what? It's really dark. How about we do this in the morning?"

"Already have it," Roane said. And he did. He'd pulled out the gurney and had Krista standing up on the part of the floor from Mom's house we had to cut out, as it had turned to stone as well. Explaining that to Brain was not easy.

Deph studied it. "What's with the duct tape?"

"Oh, that," I said, stalling for time, praying my brain cells would kick it into high gear. "Well, that is the artist's use of symbolism to denounce our cruel and violent world, where women have to patch themselves up and get back out there, wounded but still fighting for our place in this world."

"And the cheer trophy?" she asked, totally buying it.

"It's what the world expects of us. We have to be beautiful, full of energy and smiles, all while cheering our spouses on to success. There's nothing left for us. It's an homage to how much we take on while depriving ourselves of our most basic needs." I couldn't help but be impressed with my interpretation of the artist's intentions. Aka mine.

Deph turned to me, took one more look at Krista, then asked, "Did you accidentally turn your cousin to stone?"

Fuck. How the hell did she know? "Of course not. Except, yes." I bowed my head in utter shame. "I may have. What am I going to do, Deph?" I grabbed her robe with both hands and pleaded with her. "I turned my cousin to stone. You have to help me turn her back."

Deph gaped at me. No idea why. She'd nailed it. She leaned over and ran her fingertips over Krista's cheek. "You really turned her to stone?" When she realized I was touching her, she slapped at my hands and jumped back.

"Oh, right." I let her go and cleared my throat. "In my defense, she was trying to kill me at the time."

"With her cheer trophy?"

"It was close by when her murderous rage hit."

Roane had stood back to wait for the show to end. When he saw an opening, he took it. "Will we be taking her inside sometime tonight? Because you're both slowly freezing to death."

It was terribly cold. And that man was wearing a kilt. Fortunately, the wolf in him hardly noticed.

"Yes, hon," Deph said. "Sorry."

"No problem. Where do you want your cousin?"

"My room," I said, deflated. "I'll keep her there until we figure out how to reverse this."

"You sure?" Deph asked. "What if she's still in there? Like, watching us?"

"Right?" I said too loudly. It was no wonder we were besties. We thought so much alike. "It's okay, though. I don't want anyone else to have to look at her. She's kind of creepy now."

Deph shook her head. "You're wrong. She was always creepy. Not much has changed."

I loved this woman.

Roane strapped Krista to the dolly and wheeled her up the stairs, trying not to wake anyone. He put her in my room while I got reacquainted with Percy.

The vines grew not only on the outside of the house, but on the inside, too. And while we weren't sure if Deph's grandfather controlled the vines or if he somehow *was* the vines, we did know he could manipulate them at will. He could push them forward, make them flourish, bloom black roses when he so chose. He used them to protect Deph when she went into a sort of supernatural coma for six whole months after bringing her grandmother, Gigi, out of the veil. She literally brought her back to life. In a word, she was amazing, as was her grandfather.

Deph brought up my suitcase, and we sat on my huge four-poster bed.

"It feels good to be home."

She beamed at me, then quickly averted her gaze.

"What?" I asked.

"It's just, I was worried you were going home for good. I was worried you'd had enough of this town and this house and everything that's happened. To hear you call it home... it just makes me happy." She leaned forward and wrapped her arms around me.

"Hey, you. One ride per customer. You already got a hug earlier."

Though I was hardly fighting her, she laughed and let go. "Wow," she said.

I followed her gaze to the silver bracelets on my wrists. "Right? I woke up with them on the day of my trip."

"You just woke up with silver vines on your wrists? Was it..." She scooched closer and lowered her voice. "Was it Percy?"

"How could it be? They're silver. Can he manipulate silver?"

She shrugged a shoulder. "I don't know, but vines are his signature move. Speaking of which, why is my grandfather wrapping vines around your wrists?" She frowned at me. "Is there anything you want to tell me?"

I did my own signature move and rolled my eyes.

She held up an index finger to put me on pause. "Hear me out. First, you steal his picture out of the hutch and display it on your dresser like a lovesick teen."

This was true.

"Then he wraps silver vines around your wrists?" She took one of my wrists and turned it over. "Vines that don't come off? Are there no clasps?"

"Nope." I lifted it into the air to admire it. "I've worn them since that morning. But we don't know it was your grandfather, Deph." I said the words to appease her, but I could hardly contain my excitement. What if it really was him? What if he gave me the bracelets as a sort of amulet to protect me? Maybe they were keeping the warlock at bay. Making sure he didn't get too close.

Deph leaned back to assess me with a critical eye. "I know a lot of strange things happen in this house—"

"Ya think?"

"—but I find this very sus."

"I find your face sus. So, just by the by, would you be weirded out if your grandfather liked me?"

She rubbed her mouth in thought. "I'll tell you what. I'll answer that the minute you tell me everything—and I mean everything—that happened this week. I want to hear more about this warlock. And the hearse, but mostly the warlock."

"You mean the warlock who abandoned me in my forty hours of need?" That drive never got any shorter. My heart sank. I would never find a soulmate. I was in love with both a warlock—who only wanted me for my charmling powers and would probably kill me for them in a heartbeat—and a house.

"I must admit, you look exhausted."

"Really?" I smoothed my hair. It was always my hair. "Do you think Percy saw me?"

Deph laughed softly and bounced off the bed. "Get some rest. We can talk tomorrow."

"Okay, but shower first." I fell back on the soft mattress. "I missed this bed so much."

"Sleep," she said before closing the door behind her.

The bed. The covers. The smell. I loved this house. I loved

the town. I could hardly believe that at forty-five, I'd found a brand-new life. And I kind of had superpowers.

I thought about all the crazy turns my life had taken in the last few months, my lids getting heavier and heavier. When I felt a vine slip around my ankle, I smiled and let myself fall into oblivion.

Unfortunately, Mother Nature had other plans. I woke up an hour later, padded into my bathroom, and saw to her needs. When done, I looked in the mirror. I had yet to turn on the light. My hair had absorbed the humidity of the Atlantic. The image in the mirror sent my heart into my throat, and I fell back against the shower door. Definitely a sign to take one. A shower. Not a shower door.

I started the shower, then rummaged through my overnight bag until I found my essentials. Meaning my many hair care products. The finicky mop atop my head required a lot of TLC.

While showering by candlelight was a favorite pastime, I had to actually turn on a light. Mostly because the last time I tried it, I ended up in the emergency room with a bruised spleen. I didn't even I could bruise my spleen. And how did they know it was bruised? I had so many questions, but the doctor just told me to stop showering by candlelight unless I had, like, twenty. Which I did not. Thus, the lights came on.

I stood at the mirror again, this time with much more control over my hair, and quickly did my nightly routine. I wanted back in that bed. Clean body. Clean sheets. Life didn't get any better.

After throwing on a T-shirt that read *I'm too old to give amok. —Winifred Sanderson* and a pair of matching boxers, I started for the bed calling my name. Three-point-five days of driving was apparently my limit. I tossed a towel over Krista's head since she was staring straight at me, and was just about to bounce onto the bed when a framed picture on my dresser caught my attention. A framed picture of him. Percy. The man I'd been ogling for weeks who had literally died before I was born.

I stepped closer to give him my usual *Good night blooming jasmine, handsome*. A little plant humor between two alchemists. Apparently, he'd been an alchemist like me before he turned to the dark side, so we often shared little plant jokes like that. Or, well, I did. But when I looked closer at his picture, or more specifically, at his face, I froze. That niggling at the back of my neck began anew. The feeling that I'd seen the warlock before, and now I knew why. He looked very much like Gigi's departed husband. Very much like Percy. If he cut his hair and dressed all in black. Just like a warlock might do.

My lungs quit working as I stared at the picture. The same sparkling blue eyes. The same sculpted mouth. The same broad shoulders and slim waist. I didn't recognize him in Phoenix because I'd only ever seen this one photo of him, and it was grainy and taken from a distance, showcasing the car he was leaning against more than the person. But he was leaning. Arms crossed over his chest. Wicked smile softening his handsome face.

In all honesty, I doubted the picture was why the warlock looked familiar when I saw him. Thinking back, it was Defiance. They had the exact same startlingly blue eyes. And, bizarrely—because she'd never met him—they even shared some mannerisms. The way they moved. The way they walked. Their facial expressions. All so similar I couldn't believe I didn't see it before. She was his spitting image.

I didn't say anything. I didn't dare. How did Percy follow me to Arizona? I'd been told he couldn't leave the grounds. That he was stuck haunting the Goode house forever. But it had definitely been him. How?

Deciding I needed far more caffeine in my system to

process this new information, I pretended like nothing was wrong, slipped into my flip-flops, grabbed my phone, and headed downstairs. The house was dark, even in daylight. Add to that the black walls and dark furniture, and it was almost impossible to navigate in the middle of the night with no illumination, but I'd done it hundreds of times.

I paid very close attention to the vines that lined parts of the walls. I knew what they were capable of. I'd seen them move faster than the eyes could track. But Percy left me alone as I strolled into the industrial kitchen and headed for the coffee pot.

I'd gotten over trying to poison everyone in the house, including myself, so I felt safe making a pot of coffee at three in the morning. Gigi still liked it old school, making an entire carafe, claiming K-Cups just didn't taste the same. I had to agree with her.

Taking my cup with me, I sat at the small breakfast table in the kitchen. We'd spent so much time at that table. Did so much research, so much planning, trying to figure out what was happening to Defiance. And then it was my turn. Almost seven months after coming to Salem, I came into my powers, meaning the witch who currently possessed them had died before they could be transferred to a new witch. When that happened, a blood heir automatically inherited the powers, though witches all over the world believed there were no more blood heirs.

Clearly, they were wrong.

I sat there, once again contemplating my life. Where I fit. What I would do. How I would live from here on out. A drastic career change in my midforties had never been a part of the plan, but it was exhilarating.

And then he came along.

I glanced at the door that led to the basement. Deph told me she'd finally found him once in a room in the basement where his bones were buried. She said the room was always locked unless Percy wanted to let you in. Maybe a surprise attack would catch him off guard.

I stood and walked over to the door. With a shaking hand, I reached for the knob. That was when a vine sprang out of nowhere and wrapped around my wrist to stop me.

Chapter Thirteen

'Til your unsolvable murder do us part.
—Wedding vows

I stared at the vine around my wrist. While surprised, I kept my cool and tried to wriggle out of the vine's embrace. So much for a surprise attack. When I failed to free myself, I tried to turn the knob anyway. The vine slid over the doorknob as well and tightened, refusing to let me even go down the stairs. At the bottom of said stairs were three doors. The left went to Gigi's apartment. The right to Roane's. And the middle door led to a tiny room that housed Percy's bones. According to Deph, that is.

But the *pièce de résistance*, the one tidbit of information that should have clued me in days ago, was the fact that Deph said Percy couldn't speak when she talked to him. He couldn't say anything. Why didn't that click? I was so slow, I sometimes wondered if I was part sloth.

Knowing Percy wouldn't hurt me, I dropped my gaze to

the floor. Demureness wasn't my style, but he tended to bring out aspects of my personality I didn't know existed. "Please, let me in."

Vines slid out of the crack between the door and the doorframe and spread across the area, refusing me entry.

"I just want to talk." I raised my phone with my free hand, encouraging him to text. "I just want to ask you a few questions."

Nothing, but he didn't let me go, either. I'd been hog-tied.

"I can have Roane here in ten seconds," I threatened.

The vines around my wrist tightened, but just barely.

"Does Gigi know you can leave the grounds?" I waited, then asked, "Does Defiance know how amazing you are?" When I still received no answer, I raised my free hand again, this time for a very different reason. "Thank you for the bracelets. They're lovely. I didn't know you could turn the vines to silver."

The vines reached around my waist and pivoted me until my back was to the door, then they pulled me against it. While my pulse quickened with each second that passed, I still wasn't scared. Not terribly, anyway.

I closed my eyes, unable to believe Percy was the warlock. Could I be wrong about our connection? Was I reading too much into his help? When I raised my lids, all doubt evaporated.

He stood before me, his head bowed, one hand braced against the door.

I started to reach out, but another vine curled around my free wrist and stopped me. I looked up. His face was so close to mine, but his eyes were closed, his jaw working hard under the strain of his doubt.

"Thank you for helping me in Phoenix. Apple would be dead right now if not for you."

Nothing.

"Can I ask why you steered me toward helping her? Do you know her?"

He opened his eyes but kept his gaze downcast while I fought for air. He was here. In front of me. So close I could almost feel him, no matter how impossible.

I decided to change tactics. To get mean. To force his hand. "I'm in love with you," I said, blurting out the one thing that I hoped would get his attention.

It worked. He raised his gaze until it locked onto mine, the blue so bright, it looked neon. He looked like a vampire I once saw in a movie.

And as romantic as that sounded, the thought startled me. "Wait, you're not a vampire, are you?"

One corner of his full mouth rose, and he said, softly, "No. Just an asshole."

I knew it! I tried to jump up and down, but again, hog-tied. "You *can* speak," I said, astonished.

"I can now," he said, his voice so smooth it rushed over me like cool water.

I had to get a grip. I was actually talking to a departed warlock. I couldn't wait to tell Deph. "You couldn't talk before?" When he shook his head, I asked, "What changed?"

"You did. You inadvertently healed that part of me that was stolen."

"Stolen?" I asked, surprised. "By who?"

He smirked but still didn't make eye contact. "By my grieving widow."

"Gigi?" Her name sounded more like a hiss, as I was trying to whisper it, but my shock got the better of me. "Gigi stole your voice?"

His gaze had laser-locked onto my mouth, much the same way mine had locked onto his. "Trust me, it was the right thing to do at the time."

"Oh." I chewed on my lower lip a moment, then asked, "Why did you follow me to Phoenix?"

He tilted his head, still studying my mouth, before answering. When he did, that answer was a thousand miles left of what I'd expected. "To protect you."

"Oh," I said again. I so needed to expand my vocabulary. "To protect me from what?"

"From those like me," he said, easing closer. He held one arm at his side as though afraid to put both on the door behind me. As though that would be too big of a commitment. "While Defiance's spell to deflect your powers is good, there are better ones. You need to learn them if you want to be invisible to us. You both do."

"Us?"

"Warlocks."

"Right. Wait, when did I inadvertently heal you?"

"When you healed the girl."

"You've been able to speak since the landfill? Why didn't you talk to me?"

He straightened as though he was going to leave.

I panicked and said, "Please, don't."

He finally looked at me, his eyes shimmering in the low light like they were made of liquid sapphire. "Don't?"

"Don't... go. Don't disappear." I turned away, suddenly embarrassed. "You always disappear."

The vines that he controlled slid around my neck and pulled me back against the wall, tightening just enough to let me know they were there. "I'm a warlock. A dead one at that. I need to disappear for a very long time."

"Until when?" I asked, hurt. "Until I grow old and die? Will that be long enough?"

"Annette," he growled from between clenched teeth, and the sensations that washed over me felt like warm whiskey rushing through my veins. He said my name in his smooth, deep voice, and I would never be the same.

My life had changed when I came to Salem and again when I came into my powers, but never more than in that moment. No way was I letting him go now. No fucking way was I letting him go.

He pushed farther in, bracing his other hand against the wall as well, but he still couldn't touch me. Or maybe he was afraid to. What would happen?

"Can you touch me?" I asked, my voice barely a whisper.

"Not like I want to."

My lids drifted shut with his confession. "Can you try?"

"You won't like it."

"Try," I pleaded, wanting every part of him.

He slid his fingers down my arm, holding his hand steady as he grazed my skin with his nails, but all I felt was an electrifying coolness. The departed really were cold, just like in the movies, but if he thought that would deter me, he was so very, very wrong.

When I lay my head back, the vines around my neck still holding me in place, even more vines wrapped around my ankles. Glided up my legs. Pulled my knees apart, sending tendrils of pleasure racing up my spine.

That was when he dipped his hand between my legs, his touch so cold it felt hot. I gasped when he circled my clit, the fluctuation of hot and cold stirring the warmth pooling deep in my abdomen. It had been a very long time since I'd had a visitor down under, and this one showed a deftness I'd never felt before.

To my great and utter surprise, the sweet sting of an orgasm began gathering like a storm cloud inside me, swirling, building mass, promising a floodtide with its release. I felt a flush of wetness between my legs when he brushed the thumb of his other hand over my nipple, sending a shot of ecstasy straight to my core.

"Percival," I gasped, and he growled into my ear, doubling his efforts.

Only he slowed down. His strokes eased to a deliberate teasing, the leisurely pace creating slow, sensual ripples that would've doubled me over if not for the vines.

I spread my legs farther apart, coaxing the climax closer. Begging for it. But when he slid his fingers inside me, the icy pressure did all the work for me. An orgasm exploded inside me, pleasure spilling into every molecule in my body as I wiggled and whimpered in surprise.

Percy tensed as the climax pulsed through me. He pressed his head against the door over my shoulder, his breaths strained as he panted into the curve of my neck, the coolness fanning over my cheek.

After a moment, I was able to gather the senses I dropped some time back. "I just came," I said, astonished.

"Yeah, I felt it."

I leaned back to look at him. Or I tried to. I was still quite thoroughly secured to the door. "You felt my orgasm?"

He nodded, and I'd never been so happy in my life.

"Did you... did you come?"

"Through you, yes."

"Holy shit."

"Indeed."

I wished more than anything on the planet I could kiss his handsome face.

"I hate to ruin the mood," he said, ruining the mood, "but you do realize the wolf heard everything, yes?"

I laughed softly. "The wolf can bite me."

A gorgeous grin spread across his face. "Then I should probably tell you, I really like you."

I stilled at his admission, and while my heart soared like a kite in a hurricane, I decided to play down my elation for prosperity's sake. "Yeah, well, I'm the first woman you've seen in decades. Of course you like me."

"Hardly," he said with a deep, soft laugh. "Ask Gigi. She'll tell you."

Ask Gigi? Ask Gigi what? Did he have a girlfriend? "Do you have a girlfriend?"

He leaned back, his irises glistening as he stared at me. "I hope so."

A wave of heat washed over my cheeks. He touched them, his cool fingers brushing over my skin as the vines retreated back into the walls. While I'd only known the warlock for a few days, I'd been getting acquainted with Percy for months. It all seemed so surreal.

"Thank you for that," he said.

"I'm pretty sure I should be thanking you."

He grinned and leaned closer. "We could always thank each other."

Oh, hell yes, we could.

Chapter Fourteen

People keep asking what sign I was born under.
Cleary, I was born under a warning sign.
—T-shirt

Deph stomped into my bedroom at the ungodly hour of—I peeked at the digital clock atop my nightstand—eleven a.m.? I shot straight up as she threw back the long curtains that blocked the sun from the floor-to-ceiling windows, blinding me nigh for all eternity.

I squinted and blocked the sun with a hand while Deph went around the room picking up articles of clothing and tossing them onto a wingback near the windows.

"I have been clamoring around the kitchen all morning, trying to lure you downstairs with the smell of coffee, home-made cinnamon rolls, and testosterone." When I raised my brows, she added, "Roane was helping."

"Ah. So, you made cinnamon rolls?" I asked, tossing her a dubious frown.

She rolled her eyes. "It's not like last time. These are really good."

"Which is exactly what you said last time." I fell back onto the bed and pulled the covers over my head.

"But I mean it this time. C'mon." She tugged at my bedspread. "Get up already. We're dying."

"Okay, okay. I'll be down in two."

"I'm setting a timer. Two minutes."

"I meant two hours."

"Annette!"

When I laughed, she headed for the door. "Two minutes. We'll be waiting. And eff you, Krista."

I laughed again and crawled out of bed with a groan. After brushing my teeth, I threw on my best—and only—robe and went downstairs for possibly the worst cinnamon rolls ever. Admittedly, they did smell good.

Before I could sit down at the breakfast table—a table currently occupied by not one, not two, but five of our closest relatives-slash-friends—a small blond creature raced toward me and threw his tiny arms around my leg. "Aunt Netters!"

"Hey, Sammie," I said, lifting him into my arms for a proper hug. Of course, I had to pretend to hate it for my audience's sake. Deph sat at the table along with a smirking Roane, a gorgeously bohemian Gigi, a terribly handsome chief of police named Houston, and Gigi's best friend, a stunning redhead named Serinda.

"Did you come back yet?" Sammie asked, and in our world, that was a fair question.

I tapped his nose. "I did. Did you miss me?"

"Yes, but did you bring me anything?"

"I most certainly did." I reached into my robe and pulled out a finger heart, our secret code since not many Americans knew about the Korean sentiment.

He laughed, pulled his own finger heart out from his jeans

pocket, and hugged me harder. It was around that moment that my real heart melted into a quivering puddle inside my chest.

I finally turned to the people waiting at the table, some patiently, some not so much. "Hey, all!" I waved and strolled with Samuel to the coffee pot.

"I've already poured you a cup," Deph said. She was the impatient one, and torturing her was far too fun. I couldn't stop now.

I scrunched my nose at it. "I see that, but it looks cold."

"I just poured it twelve seconds ago." She patted the chair beside her. "I saved you a seat."

Ink, also known as the scruffiest cat this side of eternity, darted through the kitchen, which prompted Samuel to wiggle out of my arms and chase him.

"Be careful!" Deph called out to him. "Stay away from those stairs!"

He didn't answer, of course.

I laughed and finally took the seat beside my bestie before she stroked out. I looked from person to person. Houston with his smooth, dark skin, a humorous tilt to his mouth. Serinda with her fiery red hair and knowing smile. Gigi with her new spiked black do and gauzy dress, a look of genuine concern in her eyes. And Roane with his handsome face and wide shoulders testing the strength of the chair he lounged against. There must be something in the water in Salem. So many handsome men with wide shoulders. Someone could make a fortune if they bottled it.

"So," Deph said, diving right in before I had a chance to taste the cinnamon roll in front of me.

"So?" I asked, taking a sip of coffee instead.

"You had an interesting night."

The coffee came up far faster than it went down. I coughed for a solid minute as a warmth spread across my face.

After taking a moment to compose myself, I whispered to her, "You heard that?"

"Everyone heard that!" she said, and I suddenly understood the urgency. Sure, she wanted to know everything that had happened in Phoenix, but my having ghost-sex in the kitchen would definitely raise a few eyebrows.

I sank down in the chair, praying the floor would open up and swallow me whole. Then I remembered where we lived, and all the accidents I'd had over the last couple of weeks, and quickly banished that thought from my mind. It could really happen.

Gigi reached over and covered my hand with hers. "I didn't hear a thing, Sarru."

"That's because you moved out two days ago," Deph said.

"Oh, yeah," I said, just remembering about the big move. "How did that go?" I asked.

She drew in a shaky breath and took a good look around the room. "Since I've been in this house for a very, very long time, bittersweet."

"I'm sorry, Gigi."

"It's all good. I'm close by should you guys ever need me."

And she was. She'd moved into the apartment behind Percy. At least I knew he could still keep an eye on her.

"Did you know he was the one who followed me to Phoenix?" I had a feeling she did when she told me to get back to Salem ASAP.

Gigi nodded. "I suspected when you said he never spoke to you."

"But I thought he couldn't leave these grounds."

Deph nodded. "I did, too."

"He couldn't, and I didn't understand it either until a few minutes ago. Until I saw your bracelets." She gestured toward my bracelets, a knowing grin on her face.

I held them up. "He gave them to me, but they're silver."

Serinda moved in for a closer look. "Those are gorgeous, Sarru. So delicate. And no clasp?"

"Nope. I just woke up with them the morning of my trip. But, again, they're silver. How did he make them silver?"

Gigi gazed at me patiently, her affection making me a little uncomfortable.

"Gigi, what gives?"

"He didn't turn those to silver. You did, Sarru."

I blinked in thought a moment, then shook my head. "I was asleep when he wrapped these around my wrists."

"He does that a lot, does he?" Deph said, her surprise all kinds of adorable.

I lifted a noncommittal shoulder.

"Then you're able to perform spells even in your sleep."

"That's disturbing," I said. "Considering my history."

"I don't know," the chief said. "You haven't killed anyone yet."

That wasn't as comforting as it should have been. "So I turned them to silver?"

"Dude," Deph said, "I love your powers. We're going to be rich."

Roane chuckled, but Gigi cast her an admonishing glare as a blond streak rushed through the room, giggling maniacally. Poor cat. "Defiance Dayne, we've talked about this. We do not use our powers in get-rich-quick schemes."

"Fine, we'll get rich slowly, then." She leaned closer to me. "You really need to practice your gold spells."

Did I have gold spells? "Okay, forget the bracelets," I said, shaking out of all the thoughts spinning around my head. "How is Percival able to leave the grounds?" I asked this knowing he was listening to every word we said about him. How could he not be? He was literally the house.

"The silver on your wrists," Gigi said. "The silver you

created from, essentially, his flesh. It opened a gateway of sorts."

Serinda gasped softly, catching on. "A Gwenllian gate."

"Precisely."

I frowned. "And that means... ?"

"It means you created a gate that supernatural beings can go in and out of. It means you have to be extremely careful, Sarru. You could pull something out of the ether without even realizing it. Something we don't want on this side."

"Great." I picked up my phone and opened up my notes. "I'll just add that to the list."

"What's more," Serinda said, "there is nothing on Earth that will get those bracelets off of you. Only a spell can do that, one from a very powerful witch."

"You're stuck with them unless you can figure out the spell," Gigi added.

I cradled them to me. "I won't be looking for it anytime soon."

"Bolt cutters," Roane said, suddenly very interested in the conversation. He sat studying the bracelets, his eyes narrowed in thought.

The chief nodded. "Or an arc welder."

While I sat horrified, Gigi laughed and shook her head. "Not even those. And you are not trying either. You have to remember there's a charmling attached to them."

"They wouldn't hurt me," I said, grinning.

"Oh, I'm not worried about you, Sarru. But they need to seriously consider what would happen if they were to injure a charmling, inadvertently or not." She turned to them and raised a chastising brow. "Don't let the name fool you."

Serinda agreed. "You do not want to make a charmling angry."

Deph and I high-fived, but I sobered pretty quickly when a vine slid around my ankle. I reveled in the feel of him near me until I looked at Gigi. The beautiful woman who'd kept her granddaughter safe for decades without Deph even knowing. The stories she must have.

Guilt slipped inside the first opening it found and settled down for a long visit. "Are you okay with all of this, Gigi? I mean, he was yours first."

"Please." She waved a dismissive hand, then pinched off a bite of cinnamon roll. "He hasn't been mine for decades, sweetheart."

My stomach tingled when she called me sweetheart. She'd barely been able to remember my name for the longest, and now I was *sweetheart*. I watched her put the chunk of cinnamon roll in the chief's mouth, the look on his face priceless. Such appreciation. Such devotion. That was all I wanted. Well, that and a unicorn named Fred. "Can I just say, you have excellent taste in men, Gigi."

"I agree, Grandma," Deph said, her own mouth full of her concoction.

"So," I said, steering the conversation back to the matter at hand, "you knew Percy had followed me because he couldn't talk to me, but wasn't that your fault? He said you stole his voice." I didn't want to sound accusatory, but I really wanted to hear the entire story.

She laughed. "I did, Sarru, at his behest. Remember, he'd gone to the dark side and became... well, addicted. The black arts are hard to resist once you get a taste. He wanted to stop, but they had taken hold. They would not allow him to stop. They would not allow him to take his own life. He had no choice but to ask me and my coven for help."

"He asked you to kill him," I said matter-of-factly.

"Yes." She dropped her gaze, clearly still affected by the event.

"And his voice?" Deph asked. She laced her fingers into

Roane's as though the very thought of having to kill a loved one like that was too much to bear.

When Gigi didn't answer, Serinda took over. "We knew that he would change his mind once we started the ceremony. It's, well, excruciating."

"You were there?" I asked, surprised.

She nodded sadly. "We couldn't let him stop the ceremony once it began."

"So you stole his voice?"

"Yes," Gigi said. "It was his decision, love. We silenced him first, then..."

"Burned him in hellfire," I finished for her. The very idea of it sent a hot poker through my gut. The vine around my ankle squeezed, and I realized Percy had also wrapped a vine into Deph's free hand. She curled it into a white-knuckled fist and rubbed a leaf with her thumb.

Serinda offered us a knowing smile. "Not hellfire, exactly. Witch fire. Much hotter."

Of course it was. A tiny kernel of resentment planted itself in my heart. I had to remind myself it was his idea. He wanted them to do it. Pleaded with them to do it, from what I understood.

"But Roane says he can talk now?" the chief said.

I glanced at the traitor. He sat completely unaffected. A good thing, since it was hardly his fault he had supernatural wolf hearing.

"He said you healed him?" he continued.

"I guess. I didn't realize I did that. I had no clue I could. He did say something very interesting, Gigi."

"Just one thing?"

"Well, this kind of stuck out. He said... he said he's had plenty of opportunities to... be with someone."

"Oh, you mean his fan club?"

154

"He has a fan club?" Deph asked, her voice an octave higher than usual.

"Not officially," Serinda said. "But he was a legend in the witch world. Most warlocks are, let's say, less than desirable. A bad boy with his looks? Forget about it," she said, turning Italian.

"Even now," Gigi added, "half the women in the coven are in love with him. They've seen pictures of him and heard the stories. He's had tons of opportunities to hook up."

"Hook up?" Deph asked. "Who are you? And how could they possibly hope to hook up with a departed warlock? That is so disturbing,"

I started to answer but changed my mind. Some things were better left to the imagination.

She caught on and cast me a sideways glance. "Oh, right. I guess you'd know."

I sank farther into my chair.

"Annette," Deph said, drawing my attention to her, "can I... can I see him?"

It didn't even occur to me that his granddaughter might want to talk to him, but it certainly wasn't for me to say. I was hardly his keeper. But when her gaze slid past me and her eyes widened, I realized I didn't need to answer. And judging by the other expressions in the room—well, all but the chief's and Roane's, for two very different reasons—the warlock was standing behind me.

I stood and turned to face him. It took me a moment to find my own voice, but I finally said, "Hey."

"Hey. I should have come sooner since this interrogation concerns me. I apologize."

"No." I shook my head. "It's okay."

Everyone else had stood as well. Even the chief, though he had no idea why. Everyone stood except the wolf. He eyed Percy like he was planning to make him his next meal, but unless the wolf could live on souls, I doubted he'd be satisfied for long.

"Defiance," Percy said. Honest to God, the man looked like a supermodel. How did I score somebody like him?

Her face morphed into one of pure joy. "I wish I could hug you."

"I do, too."

"You're younger than I am."

He shrugged. "Just barely. I guess it depends on how you look at it. I was forty when I died."

I felt my eyes round to the size of saucers. I totally forgot that he was five years my junior.

Gigi tried to high-five me. "Way to go, Nannette."

I plastered my hand over my face. I knew five years wasn't that much, but I still felt like a cradle robber. Like I'd molested a child. Like I deserved to be arrested.

The chief leaned into Gigi. "Is he as good-looking as everyone says?"

The grin that spread across her face was pure wicked. "Even more so."

"Damn it. He better not want you back."

She winked at me. "I don't think that's going to be a problem."

"Sarru," Serinda said, sensing my distress, "is there anything we can do for you? You've had a rough few days."

We sat back down as Deph and her infant grandfather talked softly to themselves. "I did get myself into a bit of a pickle I was hoping you guys could help with."

"Really?" Gigi asked, her interest piqued.

"I kind of accidentally turned my cousin into a statue."

"Ah." Gigi nodded in understanding. "That's why there's a hearse in the driveway."

"Speaking of which, I'll arrange to get that shipped back today."

"When you say accidentally..." the chief said, urging me to continue.

"Well, she was about to kill me with a cheer trophy, and I just, sort of, touched her. Next thing I know, she's a statue."

All three of my current audience members leaned back in their chairs, putting as much distance between us as they could.

Great. Now I was a pariah.

Chapter Fifteen

Two minutes after being kidnapped:
ME: *blushing* so what made y'all choose me?
—True story

After everyone except Deph, Percival, and me left, I sat at the table for another hour, eating more cinnamon rolls than I had a right to, as Deph and her grandfather talked. She had more questions for him than I did, ranging from his lineage to how he got into the dark arts to how he ended up a house.

He answered most of the questions quite vaguely—as guys were wont to do—but he warned her to stay away from dark magic. And he did talk extensively about his family. His childhood. His initial powers. I basked in the information, hanging on their every word, but there was a shower out there somewhere with my name on it.

I slipped away, took a very long shower, then dressed in a warm fall sweater, boyfriend jeans—now that I semi-had one—and brown suede boots. I looked over at Deph's familiar, a black cat named Olly. Only he wasn't so much a cat as a supernatural creature who could swallow people whole. I had to admit, I was a tad wary of the thing, but he'd taken to sleeping on my bed during the day. I figured he was like a bear. I steer clear of him and he steers clear of me. Win-win.

He stopped licking his paws long enough to focus on me, and I fought the urge to pet him. He was awfully cute, though. But I had too much to do to be eaten today. Deph had invited her dads over for dinner to meet Percival, and I had the perfect meal planned, which involved three stops at three different Salem restaurants. But first, a latte from one of my ten favorite coffee shops in Salem: Spells Coffee.

The salty air smelled wonderful as I sat on a park bench to sip the delicious brew. I'd grown quite fond of Salem. As much as I loved Phoenix, I'd missed the sea. The clouds. The cool weather.

A couple sat next to me, so I scooted over a bit. Clearly tourists, they pointed at all the sights Salem had to offer while they dipped freshly baked pretzels in a chocolate sauce.

They turned to me, and the man asked, "Do you know where the Witchery is?"

I winced at the mention of my mortal enemy's shop, no matter how cool it was. "Sure. One block up on the left."

"Thanks." They finished their snacks and headed for the store.

I watched them longingly. I loved that store. I'd be there now if I hadn't been banned for life. A month or two, I could see, but an entire lifetime? That woman was never going to forgive me.

Another tourist walked up to me. "Can you show me where the witch museum is?"

I looked up to find a well-dressed man in his late forties standing over me. Feeling like a bona fide local, I pointed in the opposite direction. "The Witch House? It's just down this street, about two blocks."

He nodded but didn't bother looking in the direction I'd pointed. "But can you show me?"

"I'm sorry?"

He sat on the bench beside me. Far too close beside me. I leaned back to glare at him properly when he opened his jacket to flash me.

Oh, hell no. And yet... my gaze dropped to his crotch. What I expected to find and what I actually found were two very different things. He held a shiny black gun, and it just happened to be pointed right at me.

"Let's go."

"I promise, you have the wrong person."

"I promise you, I don't. Get the fuck up." He put a hand around my arm and jerked me to my feet, and a thousand ways of getting out of this ran rampant through my mind.

Should I scream? Isn't that what they say to do? To scream and run because the chances of a gunman actually hitting you were slim to none? It was that *slim* that stopped me. Slim was nowhere near none, and I just really didn't want to get shot. Slimly or otherwise.

We walked past the Witchery, and I wondered if I'd ever get to go inside again. I wondered if I'd die. I certainly didn't want to.

"If you could just tell me what you want..."

"Right now, I want you to shut the fuck up."

I could do that. The suit led me to an SUV with blacked-out windows and pushed me inside, and I knew enough about statistics—damn my love of procedurals—to know my chances of survival had just dropped dramatically.

I tripped and landed hard on my knees between the front and middle rows of seats. After crawling onto one of them, I turned to him. He stood at the door, but I quickly figured out we were not alone. One man sat in the driver's seat and at least one other man sat in the back seat.

The world spun around me in disbelief.

He climbed in behind me, took out his phone, then turned to face me, making sure he had my full attention. "Where's Krista?"

Krista? They wanted Krista? "I don't know. I haven't spoken to her since I left Phoenix."

The world blurred for a brief moment. It wasn't until I fell back that I realized I'd been hit. I hardly felt it, I was so stunned.

"I'm not asking twice."

I didn't dare speak.

The smile that spread across his face convinced me he really liked his job.

I glanced at the men in the back seat. One looked very much like the one who abducted me. Same crisp suit. Same perfect hair. The other... the other leaned against the door, his face pressed against the window, his hands tied behind his back, a bloodied and vomit-filled plastic bag over his head.

"Is he dead?" I asked inanely as a wave of nausea washed over me with the strange scent that filled the air.

The suit laughed. "You're quick."

My lungs turned to cement when I recognized the Bob Seger T-shirt the man wore. Brad Gaines lay dead in the back seat of the car I was currently sitting in. And I saw him. I saw his killers. I was not getting out of this vehicle alive.

Tears stung the backs of my eyes as the suit woke up his phone. He tapped on the screen, then turned the phone to me. It was a split screen, a man, tied up and gagged, on top, and a woman, same, on the bottom. My breath came out in a whoosh and tears began to run freely down my cheeks.

The suit leaned closer. "Look, we don't give a rat's ass

about your parents. We just want that bitch. Everyone else will be free to go the minute we get her."

Now why didn't I believe him? "You don't have to lie to me."

He laughed. "But that's what we call incentive. You give us what we want and we give you what you want."

"We're dead either way."

He shook his head. "It's like you don't trust me. I'm hurt."

"Just let them go and kill me." I didn't realize my parents could hear me. They both started protesting through their gags, my mom's face streaked with tears as she sobbed. My dad had a black eye and, most likely, a broken nose.

The suit grabbed a handful of hair and jerked me forward off the seat. "You're not understanding the game. See Brad over there?" After forcing my head to the right so I'd get a good look at him, he pulled me back to him. "He understood the game very well, and look where he ended up."

I couldn't concentrate. The taste of bile rose up the back of my throat as I tried to think, but my brain just wouldn't work. "I don't understand. The cops seized the money. Why do you want her?"

"First, to slice her throat and watch her choke on her own blood."

I closed my eyes at the image.

"Second, did you really think that was all the money she took? That would barely put a dent in what she took." He pulled me closer until we were nose to nose. "She stole an entire truck full. Almost a hundred million in cash. She hid the rest somewhere else and, well, we'd like it back."

"A hundred million?" There was more money? The final tally on the haul from the closet was a little over five million. And I'd turned her to stone.

"Look," I said, thinking out loud, my voice quivering as fear sank its claws even deeper into my skin, "I'll take you to her. She came with me from Phoenix. Just let my parents go and I'll take you to her."

He shook his head and looked into the phone. "Kill the woman."

"No!" I screamed, lunging for the phone.

"You don't think we followed you? We know she wasn't with you."

"I didn't say it was with me. She drove a rental to cover her tracks."

"Okay, fine." He lifted a shoulder, seemingly indifferent, but I knew better. "If you're lying, everyone dies and I go home to play Parcheesi with my uncle Raymond. If not... well, we'll just have to see."

I couldn't believe I was considering taking them to the house, yet the house—aka, Percival Channing Goode—may be the perfect place for them. If only I could make sure Gigi was in her apartment. And, goddess willing, Deph would be in her room or Roane's basement apartment. But surely Percy and Roane would protect them. Roane would hear us coming from a mile away, and Percy would know the second we walked into the house. If not sooner.

We walked into the foyer, the house eerily quiet.

The suit gave himself a moment to take it all in. Percy was something to see, that was for sure. When he'd gotten his fill, the four of us walked through the house and ended up in the kitchen. "Where is she?"

"She must still be gone. She had to run an errand, but she should be back any second."

He grabbed my hair again—he really liked my hair—and pulled me close. "If you're lying, you do not want to know the things I'll do to you. Not to mention your parents."

My phone dinged. The suit nodded, so I grabbed it from my bag. It was a message from... Krista?

He jerked the phone out of my hand and read the text.

On my way. Do you want a latte while I'm out?

He held the phone out to me. "Answer her."

I was shaking so hard, I could barely type. *I just got one, thanks.*

Your loss. Back in five.

It had to be Percy. He was texting as my cousin. I could have kissed him for his ability to hack an iPhone and his ability to sound like one of us.

The suit nodded to the driver, a man who could've been his twin if not for the size difference. The beefy man walked to the sink and filled a glass with water. When he brought it over and handed it to me, I smelled it instantly. Though I couldn't identify the exact substance, I knew it was poison. I knew it would kill me. It was the same scent I'd detected in the SUV. Had they killed Brad this way? What a horrible way to go, even for an asshole like him. Would they kill my parents the same way?

"It'll help you calm down," the suit said.

Yeah, way down.

"Drink it or I order my men to shoot your father in the head."

I bit down and, never one to mince words, asked, "Why are you killing me this way?"

The surprised look on his face was almost comical. And, oddly enough, there was a hint of respect behind his eyes. "Because Hercules over there doesn't like blood."

I nodded. Made sense. "Are you Krista's husband?"

"I am. And now I have to clean up her mess."

So, this was Daren Diaz. "I'm sorry, but you just don't look like a Daren."

He frowned at me. "Just drink."

He really didn't, though.

I closed my eyes and silently thanked the goddesses for the wonderful gifts they'd given me. My best friend. My new family. My old family. My powers. Everything I never thought I'd have—especially superpowers... and a hot boyfriend—all of it fell into my lap and I didn't deserve any of it. I squeezed my eyes shut tighter and felt tears rush down my cheek as I lifted the glass to my mouth. I downed the bitter liquid like a shot, in one massive gulp. Then I coughed for several minutes, worried I'd throw it up and have to do it all over again.

Daren seemed impressed. He glanced at Hercules, and I had to wonder if that was his real name. Hercules raised a brow as Daren sat next to me. "I have to admit, I've never in all of my years of doing this seen someone actually drink it. Not without a lot of encouragement."

His words started to run together as the toxic substance started taking effect.

"Tony?" he said into his phone. He stood and glared at the screen. "Mark? What the fuck is going on? Is that... is that a plant?"

The back door opened, and Deph walked in carrying an armful of groceries.

Daren lifted the gun toward her, but when Roane walked in behind her, a challenging glare in his eyes, Daren trained the barrel on him.

"Oh, hey, guys," Deph said. "Are you staying for dinner? We have plenty."

Her attitude threw Daren. He wasn't sure what to think, but he knew enough to keep the gun focused on Roane. It was the wrong decision. Deph put down the groceries and drew a spell on the air. The lines split open, and a bright light spilled out of them, blinding me, blurring my already blurred vision since I was dying and all.

The men couldn't see the spell, so they watched her in confusion, not sure what was going on. But they stayed like that for a really long time, like Netflix on pause.

"Bam, bitches." Deph pumped her fist. "I may not be able

to turn someone to stone, but I can damned sure incapacitate them."

When I realized the three men weren't going anywhere fast, I bent over and vomited onto the floor. Then I breathed a sigh of relief as the heavenly sound of sirens filled the air. Maybe it wasn't too late. Maybe I could be saved.

"Nette!" Deph knelt beside me. "Are you okay?"

"Can you, perhaps, get me to a hospital?"

"I can't believe you drank that. Are you crazy?"

"Hospital," I croaked.

"After everything we've been through, you just gave up your life in the blink of an eye. Did you even think of me? Of my grandfather, who happens to be head over heels in love with you?"

"Maybe call poison control?"

Gigi walked in with Samuel in tow. "Did it work?"

"Of course, but she drank poison again."

Gigi tsked me. "Nannette, haven't we talked about this?"

Samuel walked up to me, and I tried to shoo him away from the poison vomit on the floor. "Ew," he said, scrunching his adorable little nose. "Why you do that, Aunt Netters?"

"Nine-one-one?" I begged. Somebody? Anybody?

The chief ran inside then and skidded to a halt when he got a good look at the assailants. "Oh, wow, I'm going to need more men. These guys are huge. How long will they stay like that?"

"I don't know," Deph said. "I've never had to use that spell. You might want to hurry, just in case."

"Is that vomit?" the chief asked as he went around hand-cuffing the men. Hercules was giving him trouble. The man was massive and frozen in place.

"Ipecac?" I whimpered as Deph poked Daren in the face, admiring her handywork.

Gigi tossed a couple of kitchen towels over the mess I'd

made and knelt down to me. "Sweetheart, you're mortiferata. The poison won't kill you."

I straightened and gaped at her. "It won't kill me?"

"Of course it won't. You could eat poison for breakfast. Not that I would."

I struggled to my feet and realized she was right. I felt just fine. Damn it. "Why didn't anyone think to mention this to me?"

"It's in the books," Gigi said.

"Roane," the chief said, "can you just grab his arm and twist it back a little?"

Roane jumped to attention. "Sure thing." The sound of a bone cracking got everyone's attention, but we pretended it didn't.

"He's not even cold," Deph said, still poking Daren.

"Wait!" I screamed looking for Daren's phone. "My parents!" I found the phone and watched as a uniform helped my mom. My dad was off screen, the camera focused on the chair he'd been sitting in. The next instant, he appeared on Mom's screen. At least, his bottom half did. Mom jumped up and they embraced, crying. Daren must've had them in separate rooms in Dad's house. I slammed a hand over my mouth as tears fell freely.

"I'm sorry, honey," Gigi said. "We had to give Percy enough time to save your parents and Houston enough time to get the cops over there before we could come in here."

"Percival? He's there?" Of course. The plants Daren saw. I would've loved to see that.

"Why you crying, Aunt Netters?"

I laughed and bent to pick him up. "Because my parents are okay."

"Honey?" Mom said, walking up to the phone. "Are you okay?"

I sank onto the floor and sobbed. "I am. I'm so sorry, Mom."

"Annette Cheri, this was not your fault at all. Have you seen Brad?"

"Yes. He won't be conning anyone anymore."

She gasped as Dad bent toward the camera and waved. "Dad, you're hurt."

"Battle wounds. Chicks dig that shit."

Mom laughed, hugged him again, then turned back to me. "He saved us, didn't he?" she asked. "Your warlock?"

"He did," I said, my voice cracking.

"Can you thank him for me?"

"For us," Dad said.

"Absolutely."

"Ma'am," a uniform said, "sir, if you two could step out while we process the crime scene?"

"Of course. Talk later?" Mom asked.

I nodded.

"He should be back any second," Gigi said.

"Wait, how did you know I'd been abducted?"

Deph grinned, the arrogant thing almost evil. "Your bestie at the Witchery saw the whole thing. She called me instantly. And then she called the cops."

"Love called you?"

"She did. See?" She slapped my arm. "She doesn't hate you."

"Can I go back into her store?"

"Absolutely not. She said no way in hell does her helping you mean you can go back into her store."

I deflated, but overall, it was hard to be too upset.

Several uniforms came in and escorted the very stiff cartel members out of the house.

"Krista's husband said that money in the closet barely

scratched the surface of what she took. She hid tens of millions of dollars."

"Really?" Deph said. "Maybe you can connect with her and find out where it is. Like a Vulcan mind-meld."

"My cousin is the last person on earth I want to mind-meld with."

"For the kids?"

I deadpanned her. Deph's reaction to the money was hilarious. I was always the one trying to get rich quick. "What kids?"

"The ones we'll be helping when we give all of it to various children's charities. Anonymously, of course." Ah. That made more sense. She would do it for a good cause.

Two hours later, I lay in bed, suffering through a spooning. I was the little spoon. The woman at my back was four inches taller than me, but that didn't mean I had to be the little spoon.

"Deph?" I said, afraid to broach the subject.

"Yes?" she asked sleepily.

"Are we done?"

"No. I almost lost you today. You have to let me spoon you for at least thirty minutes."

I checked the clock. It had only been two minutes and thirteen seconds. I was going to die before this ended.

"Can I ask you something?"

"Thirty minutes," she said, refusing to budge.

"It's about Austin."

She leaned back and propped her head on an elbow. "What about him?"

I could hardly believe I was asking this, but it could help bring closure to my parents. And me, I supposed. "Can you search for him? I mean, for his bones? Maybe we can find out what happened to him. It's so empty not knowing."

She rolled onto her back and stared at the ceiling.

"I know it's asking a lot."

"No, not at all. I was going to ask you something, too."

I faced her and propped my head on an elbow as well. "Shoot."

Tears began to well in her eyes.

"Deph," I said in alarm. "What's going on?"

She wiped her eyes and drew in a shaky breath. "We found out why Samuel died."

"Oh."

"He had a rare form of leukemia. Something almost unheard of back in his time."

"Deph, oh my God. Wait. Why are you upset?"

"Because when I brought him out of the veil, he still had it." She pressed her lips together, then focused on me. "He still has it, and his chances of survival are less than twenty-five percent."

I pressed a hand over my mouth. "Deph, I don't know what to say."

"I'm so sorry to ask this, but can you try to heal him?"

My lids drifted shut for a few pregnant seconds before I nodded. "You know I'll try. I'll die trying, Deph, but what if I can't?"

"It's okay. I just want you to try. If it doesn't work, we can get the coven involved. Maybe they can help somehow."

For possibly the first time in our very long friendship, I pulled my bestie into a hug. She cried into my shoulder. I cried into her hair. The thick black silk was too perfect, anyway.

"We aren't gods, Nette. We don't really have a right to heal people, do we?"

"We have every right to save a child's life. Nothing will ever convince me otherwise."

Vines slid up the sides of the bed and curled around us in a sweet embrace.

"Thanks, Percy," Deph said. She sniffed and looked at me. "I guess I have to tell you now."

"Tell me what?"

She grabbed a tissue and wiped her nose before explaining. "I've already searched for Austin's bones, Nette. Weeks ago, when I was practicing."

I stilled completely, afraid to move for fear of missing something she might say. "And?"

"I can't pinpoint his location exactly. Like with Apple, something is blocking me."

"Like a spell?" I asked, confused.

"It's similar, yes, but I do know one thing."

"Okay," I said warily.

"Annette, your brother is still alive."

Afterword

Thank you for reading **MOONLIGHT AND MAGIC: A PARANORMAL WOMEN'S FICTION NOVEL (BETWIXT & BETWEEN BOOK 4)**. We hope you enjoyed it! If you liked this book – or any of Darynda's other releases – please consider rating the book at the online retailer of your choice. Your ratings and reviews help other readers find new favorites, and of course there is no better or more appreciated support for an author than word of mouth recommendations from happy readers. Thanks again for your interest in Darynda's books!

Darynda Jones
www.daryndajones.com

Never miss a new book
from Darynda Jones!

Sign up for Darynda's newsletter!

Be the first to get notified of new releases and be eligible for special subscribers-only exclusive content and give-aways. Sign up today!

Also from **DARYNDA JONES**

PARANORMAL
BETWIXT & BETWEEN
Betwixt
Bewitched
Beguiled
Moonlight and Magic
Midnight and Magic
Masquerade and Magic
Love Spells
Love Charms
Love Potions
Samuel

CHARLEY DAVIDSON SERIES
First Grave on the Right
For I have Sinned: A Charley Short Story
Second Grave on the Left
Third Grave Dead Ahead
Fourth Grave Beneath my Feet
Fifth Grave Past the Light
Sixth Grave on the Edge
Seventh Grave and No Body
Eight Grave After Dark
Brighter than the Sun: A Reyes Novella
The Dirt on Ninth Grave
The Curse of Tenth Grave
Eleventh Grave in Moonlight
The Trouble with Twelfth Grave

ABOUT THE AUTHOR

New York Times and *USA Today* Bestselling Author Darynda Jones has won numerous awards for her work, including a prestigious RITA®, a Golden Heart®, and a Daphne du Maurier, and her books have been translated into17 languages. As a born storyteller, she grew up spinning tales of dashing damsels and heroes in distress for any unfortunate soul who happened by. Darynda lives in the Land of Enchantment, also known as New Mexico, with her husband and two beautiful sons, the Mighty, Mighty Jones Boys.

Connect with Darynda online:

www.DaryndaJones.com
Facebook
Instragram
Goodreads
Twitter

Printed in Great Britain
by Amazon

17387437R00107